The Pattern of Piney Series

BRUSHED
by Hope

BOOK THREE

By Katharine E. Hamilton

ISBN-13: 979-8-9887083-1-5

Brushed By Hope
The Pattern of Piney Series
Book Three

www.katharinehamilton.com

Cover Design by Kerry Prater.

To Erin and Jack... Jarin was the perfect addition.

All Titles
By Katharine E. Hamilton

The Brothers of Hastings Ranch Series
Graham

Calvin

Philip

Lawrence

Hayes

Clint

Seth

The Siblings O'Rifcan Series
Claron

Riley

Layla

Chloe

Murphy

Sidna

The Lighthearted Collection
Chicago's Best

Montgomery House

Beautiful Fury

Blind Date

McCarthy Road

Heart's Love

The Unfading Lands Series
The Unfading Lands

Darkness Divided

Redemption Rising

The Pattern of Piney Series
Hooked By Love
Stitched By Memory
Brushed By Hope

A Love For All Seasons Series
Summer's Catch
Autumn's Fall

Mary & Bright: A Sweet Christmas Romance

Captain Cornfield and Diamondy the Bad Guy Series
Great Diamond Heist, Book One
The Dino Egg Disaster, Book Two
The Deep Dive, Book Three

The Adventurous Life of Laura Bell
Susie At Your Service
Sissy and Kat

«CHAPTER ONE»

"*I've got over twenty* teenagers sitting in my coffee shop right now, your daughter being one of them, Reesa." Jamie Bishop shouldered her phone as she swirled a plastic cup with ice, chocolate syrup, milk, and espresso. She set it on the counter. "Becca!" she called out and then went back to her conversation. "T.J. on his way? I texted him a bit ago."

"Why is Clare there?" Reesa asked. "And Theo just left, I assumed to go home. How am I so out of the loop? What is going on? Clare should be at prom."

"She was," Jamie clarified. "But instead of going to the after-prom party hosted at the school, some of the kids wanted to hang out here, the coolest place in town. And by some, I mean—" Jamie looked up as the bell above her door rang and six more teens walked inside the shop. "Oh, make that almost thirty now."

"Do you need help?" Reesa asked.

"Yes, though I don't want to interrupt Clare's night by having her mother show up."

"Hey, I'm a cool mom."

"Don't I know it," Jamie agreed. "But I don't want to step on her toes. If you think she'll be cool with it, then come on."

"Hmmm… let me talk to her real quick."

"Clare!" Jamie called out and the pretty young girl raised her head, looking in her direction. Jamie waved her phone at her. "Your mom."

Clare hopped to her feet, her sequined dress catching the lights and casting purple and turquoise shimmers on anything she passed. Jamie's heart squeezed at seeing how lovely Clare looked for her first big night in Piney. She'd had a homecoming dance at one point, but prom was a big deal to teenagers. At least, it had been when Jamie was in high school. And she never remembered a place kids could go after the prom to avoid the parties taking place all over town. She loved being the safe haven, fun spot, or relaxing bungalow in which the kids chose to abide. She especially loved Clare and loved the friendship she and Reesa Tate, Clare's mother, had formed over the last several months. Within just a short time, the two women felt like family. And Theodore Whitley, her childhood friend, had fallen head over heels in love with Reesa, which Jamie found highly entertaining to watch. Clare took the phone. "Hey, Mom. What's up?"

"Jamie sounds swamped. Would you be cool if I came up there to help her? I don't want to ruin your night."

"Oh." Clare paused and thoughtfully considered her feelings on the matter. "No, that's fine. She could use the help. We sort of swooped in on her en masse."

"Sounds like it. Okay, as long as you're sure."

"Yeah, it's not a problem." Clare turned towards the door at the familiar jingle. "You sent Theo already?" she asked.

"No," Reesa replied. "Jamie texted him a honey-do list apparently."

"That makes sense. He has tons of bags of snacks."

"Awe, really?" Reesa's voice softened. "That was sweet of him."

"Mom, stop. He probably *just* left our house. You can come gush over him here."

"Oooooo, you're right. I can," Reesa's voice chimed over the phone. "Okay, go have fun. Tell Jamie I'll be there soon."

"Will do." Clare hung up and handed the phone back to Jamie. She nodded a greeting at Theo on her way back to her table with her friends.

"You're a lifesaver." Jamie grabbed the grocery bags from his hands and bustled back behind the counter. Theo followed her. "Wash your hands and grab an apron."

"I wasn't staying."

"Your wife is headed over here, so you might as well." Her eyes widened at her slipup. "I mean, your *girlfriend*. Oops." She giggled as Theo's stoic face blanched. "Didn't mean to scare you." She tugged an extra apron off the side wall and tossed it at him.

"Didn't scare me," he mumbled, slipping it over his head. He walked over to the sink and washed his hands. "What do you want me to do?"

"Chips in big bowls." She pointed to underneath her prep counter. "I'm going to start whipping together some panini sandwiches and we'll make some trays. After the chips, start washing fruit. Reesa can fill drink decanters when she gets here."

Theo quietly obeyed and Jamie appreciated his willingness to jump in alongside her and help. Dependable, loyal, and steadfast, their friendship had withstood the test of time, hurt, and change. She loved seeing Theo and Reesa blossoming into a serious relationship and his connection with Clare; she only hoped Theo wouldn't wait too long to make an official profession of that love. "Clare looks so pretty tonight," Jamie whispered. "I've noticed several of the boys keeping a close eye on her, not just Teddy Graham."

Theo grunted and Jamie smiled before swatting him with a hand towel. "Daddy Bear." She chuckled. "None of them have been disrespectful," she assured him. "Besides, we both know Clare can hold her own when it comes to taking care of herself."

"She comes by it honest," Theo remarked, looking up as Reesa burst through the doors. Her smile brightened the room as her eyes sought out her daughter. Clare gave her a small wave and Reesa nodded in greeting. She walked towards the counter and paused, her cheeks flushing pink. "Theo..." she gushed. "You are rockin' that apron. Wow." She fanned herself as she watched him for a moment.

"See how you pull one off." Jamie tossed another extra apron to her friend with a wink and nudged Theo aside with her hip as she scooted down the counter to reach for her panini grill. "We've got you on decanters. I've got some passion pink lemonade and berry infused water planned." She pointed and Reesa stepped into the small work area.

"I can handle it," Reesa assured her. "Thanks for doing this, Jamie. I'm glad the kids have somewhere they can go to hang out and have fun without... shenanigans."

"Oh, they still do that. I heard one of them discussing a pasture party."

Theo's back stiffened. "Where?"

"I don't know. I haven't overheard that much information yet."

"That needs to be shut down," Theo mumbled.

"Well, play it cool, T.J. Just keep your ears peeled and maybe we'll overhear the location. Then we can call the sheriff."

"What is a pasture party?" Reesa asked, curious as to why such a thing would need the sheriff involved.

"Oh, you know, find an empty pasture away from all grownups and in the middle of nowhere so they can drink alcohol and party," Jamie explained.

"What?" Reesa's eyes widened. "I've never heard of such a thing. Clare better not go." Reesa, concerned, looked at Theo.

"She wouldn't," he told her. "This is more her style."

"Agreed," Jamie chimed in. "You don't have anything to worry about with her."

"Has she been canoodling with Teddy?" Reesa asked.

"Actually, no." Jamie, just as confused as Reesa, shrugged her shoulders. "They haven't spoken much. Not sure if they're arguing or just mingling."

"That's odd. They were both super excited about tonight."

"Who knows." Theo slid the bowls of chips onto the counter and began washing fruit. Reesa nervously popped blueberries in her mouth as he washed them. He paused a moment and grabbed her hands, her nervous eyes looking up at him. "She's fine," he whispered. "And having fun. Don't worry, okay?"

Reesa nodded, accepting the quick and reassuring hug he gave her.

"Besides, how's she going to slip out now when we're all here?" Jamie concluded. "She wouldn't get one foot over the threshold without one of us runnin' her down."

"And I love that." Reesa smiled. "I'm thankful for the both of you being her hidden watchdogs."

"I don't know about hidden." Jamie thumbed over towards Theo as he offered a hard stare at a loud boy making crass jokes. The boy instantly quieted when he caught Theo's eye. The women bit back a smile.

"I love the power he has in just a single look," Reesa whispered to Jamie.

"He's always been that way." Jamie pressed down on the grill and waited a minute before lifting and scooping out the hot sandwich. She sliced it, placing two halves on a tray. She lifted the other two grills and did the same. Soon, she had an entire stack of turkey Italian paninis. She placed them on the counter by the chips and the full fruit platter Theo had thrown together. She would have organized the fruit into a pretty display, but when she started to tweak his efforts, she received one of those silent looks from Theo as well and stopped her attempts. She grinned sheepishly and confidently slid his tray towards the other food.

She raised her voice. "Food is ready!"

Several heads popped up and feet scrambled as a line began to form. Teddy Graham, Clare's best friend and possibly crush, walked up in line. "Thanks for all this, Ms. Jamie."

"Of course." Jamie smiled as he greeted Reesa and genuinely took time to interact with Clare's mom. The boy was a sweetheart and a true friend to Clare, and Jamie was glad Clare had someone like him to hang out with. She was curious, however, to see that the two of them hadn't interacted for much of the evening. Teddy always had stars in his eyes when Clare was nearby. Tonight, though, he seemed aloof towards her. She saw Clare closely watching his interaction with Reesa, her face hiding her feelings.

"I think she's mad at him," Theo grumbled under his breath, as he stepped up beside Jamie.

"Why do you say that?"

"I can just tell. She and Reesa get the same look in their eyes when they're upset. It's a distrust of sorts. Clare is looking at him like she doesn't trust him."

"But why?"

"I don't know. How would I know?" Theo looked baffled. "I just got here ten minutes ago."

"Well, you seem to be the expert on reading them. I was just asking."

"And why are we so invested in what is probably teenage drama?" He grunted in distaste at himself and Jamie stifled a laugh.

"Because I am nosy, you are protective, and Reesa is paranoid. We all have our reasons."

"Good point," he agreed.

Clare walked up and began fixing a plate. "Hey, beautiful!" Jamie greeted, lightly brushing a finger over one of the curls that framed Clare's face. "You look so pretty tonight."

"Thanks." Clare placed a handful of strawberries on her plate.

"Was prom fun?"

"Yeah. I mean, the music was a little lame, but I enjoyed dancing."

"Good. You having fun now?" Jamie asked curiously. "Or should I turn up some jams?" She began dancing behind the counter and hip-bumping a serious Theo, and Clare giggled at his discomfort.

"I think we're good. I think most of them are going to head out soon anyway."

"Oh?" Jamie asked. "Why? See, I knew I should have had you pick up a karaoke machine." She punched Theo's arm.

Clare smirked as she shrugged. "There's some kind of party a lot of them want to go to."

"Well, what about you?" Jamie asked, nonchalantly, hoping she wasn't coming across as prying.

Clare took it in stride as she filled a glass of lemonade. "Not my thing. I'll probably just go home."

"Teddy taking you home?" Theo asked.

Clare looked up at him and quietly shook her head. "I was going to see if I could ride with you or mom, if that's alright?"

"He's going to the party?" Jamie asked in a whisper.

Clare nodded, her distaste with the situation evident. "I think he feels like he has to."

"Why?" Theo asked.

"I don't know. He said he had to go for a little while at least. He was annoyed that I didn't want to go. I think he wanted to use me as his excuse to leave early or something."

"He could just leave when he wants to," Theo replied. "Or better yet, not go."

Clare held up her hand to calm the annoyance that seeped from Theo's tone. Her eyes held disappointment at the unfolding of the evening, and Jamie slid a cookie from her display case onto Clare's plate. "Hang in there, sunshine."

"You let me know when you're ready to leave," Theo told her, and she nodded in quiet agreement as she walked off to rejoin her friends.

"Odd that Teddy wants to go to a pasture party," Jamie whispered.

Reesa walked up. "Okay, so what's going on? Did you get the spill? I was trying to be busy washing dishes."

"Teddy wants to go to some big party. Clare doesn't. She's riding home with y'all, but she's aggravated at Teddy for going, and he's annoyed with her because she isn't."

"Atta girl." Reesa patted Theo. "Would you bring her home? I don't want to take away all her cool points by going home with her mom."

"I got her." Theo nodded.

"I just love you." Reesa kissed his cheek as she slid into his side and looped her arm around his waist. "Thank you."

Jamie rolled her eyes. "Alright, if y'all are going to get all cute up in here, you both need to go. I'm going to have a mess to clean up here soon."

"How about Theo takes Clare home and I stay to help you clean up?" Reesa asked. "Whenever the crowd starts breaking up."

"Plan accepted." Jamie high-fived her friend, then they both looked to Theo for his agreement, and he nodded. "Looks like that might be now." She tilted her head in the direction of the teens, and several were ragging on a handful that remained seated. Clare stood and walked towards Teddy. Her hands gently rested on his arm as she whispered to him. He shook his head and said something back, Clare reluctantly releasing her hold. She watched him leave with the bulk of the crowd, her eyes disappointed. She looked to the adults and Theo took his cue.

"See you." Reesa kissed him and held his face in her hands. "Thanks."

Theo took a moment and stared down at her, his hands resting on her hips. He kissed her tenderly on the lips, rested his forehead against hers for a moment, and then slipped away to make his ride offer to Clare. Jamie and Reesa watched as Clare hopped to her feet, more than ready to leave. "She's peopled out," Reesa whispered.

"And frustrated with Teddy."

"Should I call his parents?" Reesa asked. "What's the standard protocol on this?"

"As soon as Clare leaves, I'm going to quiz the kids on where the party is at. I'll make the calls to have it shut down."

"Good."

Jamie watched as Theo and Clare climbed into his pickup truck and backed out of the parking lot. As soon as they had left, Jamie banged a spatula on the counter, and the remaining ten or so teens looked up. "Alright, which one of you wants to spill the beans?"

^

The plans were simple enough. He was used to working on structures, new-builds, and businesses by now. Theodore Whitley knew what he wanted, and he'd sketched detailed drafts. The engineer had already approved them and now it was Jason's turn to tackle the next phase. The building phase. He'd always been good with his hands. From an early age, he had helped his dad build all sorts of fences, barns, and pens on their family farm. Now, he focused on houses, buildings, decks, and the like. Theo's project, however, was a bit different. The addition to his current business would be right in the middle of Piney, and not only did it need to look nice so Jason's reputation would continue to scale upward, but because it was a new business venture for Theo. Failure was not an option for either of them. Jason needed the work. Sure, he did okay, but with two failed marriages, the most recent one leaving an expensive mess in its wake, he needed another project that showcased his business. Building such a project from the ground up made his blood hum. Big projects tended to do that. Hard projects. He'd never built such a structure like this one. Yes, he'd built a few buildings around town, but a carwash was a whole new ball game. He could do it, though. It would take a bit of time, but he knew he and his crew could tackle it.

He and Theo went back to their high school days. Not exactly enemies, but not quite friends either. They had competed in sports, academics, girls... but oddly, over the last several months, they'd come to be friends, or Jason thought they had. They'd hung out on occasion, thanks to Reesa, Theo's new girlfriend, and Jamie, their mutual friend that also grew up in Piney.

His cell phone buzzed in his pocket, and he glanced at his watch before lifting the phone to his ear. "Hey there, Red. Little late in the evening for you to be calling me."

"Hi, Jason." Jamie Bishop's familiar voice flooded the line and held a touch of concern.

"What can I do for you?"

"Well, I was hoping you could step outside your door and take a look around."

Jason smirked. "Got a surprise for me?" he flirtatiously teased.

"If you call thirty drunk teenagers a surprise, then yeah, sure," Jamie continued.

"Wait. What?" Jason hurried to his front door and swung it open. All that faced him was darkness and a few stray fireflies.

"You see anyone? Hear anyone?"

"No. Why?"

"Apparently a group of kids were going to throw a pasture party after prom. I was thinking, well... your place has the reputation of being a hot spot, so I figured maybe they'd snuck out there."

"I haven't had a pasture party on this land since I was in high school."

"Ah, but Jason Wright is the coolest," Jamie reminded him. "I imagine they thought it would be fun."

He sighed and ran a hand through his dark hair. "I'll go have a look. Any idea where on my family's property?"

"Nope. I just assumed it was yours. May not be. I'm calling Charlie, too, to keep an eye out at his place. Y'all live the furthest out, so I figured they'd aim for that."

"What about near Theo? He's got the woods. Maybe they decided to hide back there at that old cemetery."

"Would you want to go to a cemetery at night?" Jamie asked doubtfully.

"Good point." He strutted down his stairs and shushed her in the phone so he could hear. He heard a faint whistle amongst the wind-tossed leaves and then a hint of laughter. "Well... I credit you again, Jamie. You literally do know everything that happens in Piney. Sounds like my place is the hot spot."

"Really?" Jamie's voice lifted. "Good. I'll call the sheriff."

"Whoa now. let me go talk to them and chase them off the place. I don't see why we need the sheriff involved."

"Because they need to be scared out of their minds," Jamie scolded. "So that they won't even think about doing something this dumb again. Are you sure they're out there?"

"Yep. I heard them. I'd say they're in the back corner near the creek. You know that little path off 1069?"

"Yep."

"That'd be my guess."

"Got it. Thanks."

"Hey," He interrupted her abrupt dismissal. "Reesa's girl isn't out there, is she?"

"No. She didn't go."

"Alright. Good deal."

"Looking out for her?" Jamie asked.

"Figured you were, but just making sure."

"I am. And for all the others. This is how stupid accidents happen. I'm calling the sheriff now, just so you know."

"Got it. Thanks." He hung up and set the phone aside. He'd been that kid in high school, throwing the big party that everyone wanted to attend. He'd fed on that thrill for years. Did he get in trouble? You betcha. Did it stop him from doing it again? Not at all. He hoped the kids in his pasture were smarter than he had been. He doubted it, but he hoped. He'd made some pretty unwise choices over the years. Some were the result of rebellion against his parents, some were because he was just plain stupid, and some were just a misjudgment on his part, like his two marriages, but that was neither here nor there at the moment. He sat on his porch steps and soaked in the late-night breeze. Within ten minutes, he saw the red and blue flashing lights of a squad car and heard the panicked screams and whistles, car engines, and the like dispersing. He smirked, remembering the thrill of the chase. A few would get caught and taken to their parents with a severe warning from the sheriff. Those not caught would head to the nearest friend's house and lie for one another when parents asked too many questions. And then there'd be a few unlucky ones who'd be ducked down in the tall grass to wait it out and be stuck or abandoned until morning. With no sympathy, Jason stood and walked back into his house and shut the door closing out the remaining sounds of disrupted teenagers.

He awoke to the incessant ring of his cell phone instead of his alarm. The time read a little after five in the morning and he immediately disliked the caller on principle. When he saw Jamie's name pop up on the screen, his frustration fled, as he knew she would not be calling if it wasn't urgent or serious.

"Red..." he greeted. "You're starting to make a habit of calling me."

"Jason. Hi. I hope I didn't wake you."

"You did, actually, so let's hear why."

"You're not as grumpy as Theo was, so I'll take it." Jamie's keys echoed over the line as she unlocked her coffee shop, and he could hear her starting her day. "You have any kids left on your property?"

"I have no idea. I've been asleep, remember?" Her silence worried him. "Why? What happened? What's wrong?"

"Teddy Graham never made it home last night. His parents, Reesa, and Clare... heck, all of us, are doing our best not to freak out that he's missing. You seen him?"

"No." Jason hurried towards his closet and grabbed the first pair of jeans he could find. "I'll go check the hay barn. That used to be one of the hideouts back when we were in school. Maybe he got left behind and spent the night with the skunks."

"Thanks. Keep me posted, please."

"Sure thing. Let me know if you hear anything too."

"Will do." Jamie hung up and Jason hurriedly buttoned his shirt on his way out the front screen door. It slapped behind him like the crack of a whip as he rushed towards his truck. He'd drive around his property and check the old hiding spots to see if there were any other stragglers besides Teddy. He hoped he didn't find any.

    As he reached the party spot, he only noted some empty beer cases, a few cans scattered here and there, and a high heel dislodged Cinderella-style as a young girl fled for fear of being caught. He picked up all the loose articles and tossed them in the back of his pickup as Charlie Edwards' truck turned up the small drive off 1069. He rolled down his window and spotted Billy Lou Whitley in the passenger side.

"Any sign of him?" Charlie asked.

"Not yet. This is the first place I've come to. You have any on your property?"

"A couple ran through last night, but they seemed to have met rides on the other side, because they didn't linger," Charlie explained.

Billy Lou leaned forward to meet his gaze. "We'll check your barn; you check the hen house and old cow pen."

"Sounds good." Jason saluted to her authority, and they headed in opposite directions through his pasture. He rumbled to a stop at the old cow pens and didn't see anything amiss. He listened for a moment, appeased that no teens sought shelter there. He pulled up near his house and hopped out of his truck. The chicken coop, or hen house, as Billy Lou called it, was a stone's throw away from his front door. He'd built it there on purpose as he checked for eggs twice a day. He hadn't yet this morning, considering it was just now pushing six, but all seemed quiet in the interior. He opened the wooden door to the soft clucks of his hens and squinted in the dark. He flicked on a flashlight and startled at the slumped figure at the back of the coop. A shiny black shoe and black tuxedo shifted at the sudden uproar of the chickens and Teddy Graham opened his eyes.

"Boy, do you have some explaining to do." Jason bit back a grin at the sore sight of a miserable Teddy Graham, and he motioned over his shoulder. "How about you come out of here and tell me what you're doing in my hen house?"

Too miserable to be afraid, Teddy climbed to his feet, shook off his suit jacket, and followed Jason out into the early dawn. "Sorry, Mr. Wright." Teddy's head hung low as he shuffled towards Jason's house with reluctant steps.

"You have a lot of people out looking for you right now."

"I do?" Surprise lifted Teddy's gaze.

"You're a teenager, not known for shenanigans, and you didn't come home last night. Did you think people *wouldn't* look for you?"

Teddy shrugged. "I didn't really think about it."

Jason smirked. "I suppose you didn't. Billy Lou and Charlie are searching my property and his as we speak. Reesa, Clare, and Theo are out looking for you. Your parents are out and about trying to think of where you've run off to. And Jamie Bishop has set the entire town on a search party for you."

"Wow." Teddy's face flushed in embarrassment.

"Yeah, so what are you going to say when they find you?" Jason asked.

Teddy shook his head. "I have no idea. That I was stupid."

Jason tilted his head back in forth and weighed the boy's words. "It's a start, but not near apologetic enough. Maybe grovel a bit more when you say it."

"You aren't mad at me for being in your chicken coop?"

Jason laughed and slapped an encouraging hand on his back. "Boy, I have woken up in odder places than that. I also know the exact feeling you're experiencing. I'm not mad at you. I feel sorry for you for what lies ahead for the next few days. People are going to make you feel really bad about your lack of judgment. You'll feel bad already, but you've lost some trust with your parents and your friends. It's going to suck for a bit, but you're a good kid, Teddy. I imagine you'll win them back over. Unless you're as stupid as I was and continue to repeat the bad choices, then you just lose them altogether. I recommend not taking that route, by the way."

Teddy studied him for a moment and silently nodded, rubbing a hand over the back of his neck. "It was a stupid idea. Clare told me not to go to the party."

"So why did you?"

Teddy looked out over the pasture and sighed. "I was invited."

"That simple, huh?"

"When you haven't ever been invited because you're 'the good kid,' then yeah... I guess it was that simple. Sounds silly now."

"And was it as fun as you thought it'd be?" Jason asked.

"No." He looked at his dust-covered dress shoes.

"Yeah, it never really is." Jason pointed to his truck. "How 'bout I take you home?"

Nodding, Teddy climbed inside the truck as Jason sent a text to Jamie to alert the troops that he'd found Teddy and that he was fine. He'd let the boy fill in the details on his own. He let Teddy stew in his seat during the drive home, knowing full well how he felt. Crummy, embarrassed, duped, and also a bit disappointed. In himself, in the situation, and even in the fact that the party wasn't what he'd hoped it would be.

He pulled behind Teddy's mother's minivan in the driveway of their brick two-story home and shifted his truck into park. The front door swung open, his mother clearing the front steps in one leap as she sped towards them. "Ready?" Jason asked.

Teddy groaned under his breath. "Do I have a choice?" He looked at Jason, who shook his head. "That's what I thought. Thanks for the ride."

"You're welcome. And Teddy?"

"Yes sir?"

"Stick with being a smart kid, okay? It's better in the long run."

The teen gave a brief nod before he folded out of the truck and accepted the frantic hug of his mother. She gave Jason a tearful nod of thanks as she immediately withdrew from her son and held his face in her hands. No disappointment on her face, just relief and love. The boy really didn't know how good he had it.

CHAPTER TWO

She brushed the last stroke of paint over the canvas and leaned back on a contented sigh. That was that. Finished. Finito. El fin. Das Ende. Jamie didn't like endings. She liked beginnings. The fresh squirts of color on her pallet. The smell of clean bristles on her brushes. The blank canvas in front of her. New. Fresh. Inviting. Endings were just duds. Sure, she felt accomplished in completing another painting she would never show anyone, but it was over. The thrill of mixing colors and textures had now officially been snuffed out. She admired her work. The lighting was captured quite well, she thought; the rays shining through the leaves of the trees falling in speckled glitter upon the serene pond. Should she add a duck? That question had plagued her throughout the entire painting of the scene.

She stood from her stool, walked to the other side of the room, and glanced back at the painting. No. No duck. The scene was complete as it was. Peaceful, serene, and warm. She liked it. Pleased with herself, she gathered up her messy brushes and carried them over to the sink. She'd let them soak in turpentine for a few minutes before rinsing out the oil-based paint. She scrubbed her hands beneath warm water with lye soap before applying her routine amount of lotion. She looked around the room at the stack of canvases of all shapes and sizes leaning up against the walls, chairs, racks, and steps. The small room off the back of her coffee shop had served as her hidden studio for over a decade. Only Theo really knew it was stuffed away in the back, though he'd never dared venture past the threshold. He was the only friend who knew much about her painting hobby. Well, other than Reesa now. And Charlie, Billy Lou, Jason, and Clare... one painting, that's all they really knew. She'd gifted Charlie Edwards a painting of his childhood home. They didn't know she had an entire room full of them. Reesa did, but she'd sworn herself to secrecy at Jamie's request. She wasn't sure why she didn't want people to know she painted. Her parents knew. After all, they were the ones to pay for all the art classes she took in the summers growing up. But they'd moved to Mississippi not long after she graduated high school and never quite understood her desire to stay in Piney, much less not to attend college. For her art, for business, for anything, really.

She'd taken the necessary training to be a barista, as well as a few night classes to learn more about business, and also through trial and error, created her coffee shop built mostly on hopes and wishes. Thankfully, that was enough to get her started, and her sheer will and determination helped it build into a successful business that provided her a nice, comfortable living while allowing her to visit with the town, and the people in it, whom she loved. Her art was her outlet. Her escape. Her way of channeling some of her leftover energy after a long day at work. And it calmed her enough that she could now go home, which was upstairs in the loft above the coffee shop, and rest before she opened her shop in an hour. Her cell phone dinged, and she glanced over. Jason Wright's name lit up and despite the fact she knew he was out of her league, she let her fanciful heart leap at the sight of it. In high school, there was never a moment she hadn't wished Jason Wright would notice her, but, Jamie didn't exactly hang out in the same crowd as Jason. He was one of the biggest heartthrobs, athletes, and troublemakers in their youth, which naturally, made him the apple of every young girl's eye, Jamie included. But instead of being friends, Jamie was more of the "Hey, can I copy your notes?" girl. She couldn't even remember how many times he had sweet-talked her into sharing her chemistry notes. And she'd handed them over with a heart-felt sigh and longing.

Jason had notified her earlier of Teddy's safe return, and relief had settled her heart enough that she was able to come and finish her painting. She had yet to talk to Reesa about Clare's feelings on the matter. The poor girl had been terrified that something had happened to her best friend and didn't sleep a wink the entire night. She hoped Clare would rest today.

Jamie walked out of her studio and into the shop. She could use a half hour to prop her feet up and close her eyes for a bit before handling the morning rush, but when she gazed about her cozy coffee shop, the excitement for a new day and the smell of coffee grounds had her donning her apron and getting started earlier than her norm. A tap on the door had her looking up and she realized she hadn't read the message from Jason on her phone. But there he stood, in the morning sunrise, looking as handsome as always, beckoning for her to come open her door.

"Morning." She held the door open, and he waltzed inside with confident, long-legged strides and a touch of swagger that had always made her knees weak. *And every other woman's too*, she reminded herself. "Why are you knockin' on my door so early?"

"You didn't answer my message," he pointed out before flashing his charming smile. "I was going to come sweet-talk you."

She playfully patted her messy bun and straightened her apron. "Well, let a girl prepare herself, Jason, before you go to all the trouble."

He laughed and sauntered over towards her order counter as she locked up behind him. "I didn't want to head back home after dropping Teddy off and I don't have to be at Theo's garage until eight, so I was hoping I could come and bug you until then."

"You barely caught me. I was about to head upstairs to my couch for a little rest before the day started."

"Oh." He looked disappointedly at her shop and then met her eyes. "Well, I can mosey on down to the diner. The old gentlemen might let me sit in on their morning routine of gossip and burnt coffee."

Jamie smirked. "I doubt it. You're not old enough yet to sit at the table of wisdom. They'd boot you out and probably even spank you for your audacity. Besides, I opted out of resting when I realized I could just take the extra time to prepare some goodies. You're welcome to grab a stool." She motioned to one of her side bars and he walked over and carried one with ease towards the counter to watch her busy herself in preparation. "How was Teddy?"

Jason grinned. "Oh, kickin' himself for being dumb."

"Did he say why he went?"

"Oh, to be cool, I guess. The "cool" kids asked him to go, and he normally doesn't get asked. Something about how he wondered what it would be like to go." He shrugged as if that feeling were foreign to him, which, Jamie thought, it probably was. Jason had always been the guy throwing the parties, not the person left out like her. Like Teddy. She understood Teddy's feelings completely. She remembered wishing to be invited to certain parties. Even if they weren't her idea of fun, just to be asked would have made her feel good. It seemed silly now, as she looked back on it, but the feeling of being included was more important to her back in high school. Thankfully, she had Theo. He was always included, but hated it, so they'd spend time together eschewing the typical high school societal structure and hang out on their own, mostly at Billy Lou's house.

"You talk to Reesa yet?"

"No. I imagine she will be here in a few. Last I had was just a blip about being relieved Teddy was safe."

"The kid has it good. I don't know why he felt the need to party it up."

"Why did you ever feel the need to?" Jamie challenged.

Jason pondered her question. "I think it's a little early for me to delve into high school me, Red. I was a messed up kid looking for approval in all the wrong ways back then. But I get your point."

She slid him a cup of coffee across the counter, and he nodded his thanks as he took a sip. His eyes closed for a moment as he savored that first sip, that warm beginning of a new day. "Gah, there ain't nothing better than that first sip, is there?"

She smiled. "Nope."

"Poor kid looked like he could have used a coffee or two. I don't know if he partook in any of the alcohol from the party, but a sleepless night with the hens had definitely taken its toll on him."

Jamie couldn't help but chuckle. "Oh, Teddy Graham..." She shook her head.

"And I doubt he'll be able to return that rented suit he had on either."

"Lesson learned, hopefully." Jamie sifted through her mixing bowls until she found her favorite ceramic and began tossing ingredients inside it to make a batch of muffins.

"How do you do that?" Jason asked.

"Do what?"

"That." He nodded towards the bowl. "You're not even measuring. What are you making?"

"Oh." She shrugged. "Muffins. The base batter is pretty much the same for whatever I decide to throw in there, so it's easy to mix together."

"But you're not measuring."

"I can eyeball it. I've done it a million times."

He eyed her curiously.

"I don't have to measure, unlike you," Jamie pointed out. "Mr. Carpenter. By the way, you and T.J. going to tell me what you two are cooking up over at the garage?"

"Not for me to say. Theo will have to share that news."

"Is it a car wash?" Jamie asked and then laughed at his guilty but surprised expression at her accuracy.

"W-what? How did you know?"

"Because Reesa has wanted one from the moment she moved here, and Theo is hopelessly in love with the woman. It doesn't take a rocket scientist to figure that one out." Jamie grinned. "I love seeing him so chummy over her. He deserves to be happy."

"As do you. I'm honestly surprised you and Theo never matched up over the years."

Jamie's face blanched. "Why on earth would you think we would?"

"Well, you're good friends, both single..." He trailed off. "You mean to tell me nothing ever happened between you two?"

"No." Shocked, Jamie adamantly shook her head.

"Huh..." He seemed genuinely surprised, but accepted her answer.

"I never dated anyone in Piney. Well, minus Billy Lou Whitley for her hospital galas," Jamie clarified.

"And I bet she is hard to beat."

Laughing, Jamie nodded. "That she is." A tap on the door had her glancing up and Jason spinning around on his stool. Reesa and Clare stood on the other side of the glass door, Reesa begging with her hands clasped together for Jamie to let her in. Jamie slid her key ring to Jason. "Do you mind? It's the yellow one."

He sauntered over to the door and unlocked it. Reesa and Clare bustled inside, Clare pausing a moment to wrap her arms around Jason in a tight hug. The act surprised him, and he stood awkwardly with his hands raised. "Thanks for finding him." She released him, walked over towards one of the bars and grabbed a stool of her own, slumping her elbows on the counter and barely keeping her eyes open.

"Goodness, have you two slept yet?" Jamie asked, as Jason walked back over and handed her the keys.

"No," Reesa whined. "Clare refuses to until she sees Teddy."

"So I can slap him," Clare announced. "And maybe punch him. Or hug him. Or just ignore him. I have no idea yet, but I want him to know I'm mad."

"I wouldn't go for the hug then," Jason recommended.

Reesa rested a hand on his shoulder in thanks for finding their friend before she turned curious eyes to Jamie. "What are you two up to this early?"

"This one came begging for company." Jamie nodded in Jason's direction, and he grinned, his hands wadding up a napkin and keeping his fingers busy.

"Oh, really?" Intrigued, Reesa slid onto a free stool. "Well, you found the best."

"I agree," Jamie complimented herself and winked in Clare's direction as she placed a saucer with an oversized cinnamon roll steaming in the middle of it right under the girl's nose. Clare's tired face relaxed into a lazy smile as she began pulling apart the sweet bread and munching.

"I had an early morning, as you know," Jason continued. "And I don't have to meet with Th—" He changed his wording quickly when he realized he was about to slip a secret. "*The* client I'm to meet with until eight. So, I came begging for company and coffee. Double whammy. Red's kind enough to oblige."

"I haven't even seen Theo since late last night." Reesa ran a hand through her unkempt hair and heaved a tired sigh. "He was worried sick about Teddy and had the luxury of driving around with Teddy's dad until four this morning. Clare and I stayed at the cabin just in case Teddy called or showed up."

"Heard him tell his momma that his phone died," Jason replied. "So he just waited it out until morning."

"I hope he has feathers in his hair for weeks," Clare mumbled. "No doubt he'll be grounded."

"We'll see." Reesa placed a hand on Jamie's and gave a friendly squeeze when she set a frothy cup of java in front of her. "You're the best. And we will be the best for Teddy, too. No doubt he feels crummy. We need to show him that we love him, despite his serious lack of judgment."

"Speak for yourself," Clare muttered.

Jamie's brows lifted at the girl's sour response, her concerned gaze drifting back to Reesa. Reesa shrugged her shoulders as if she wasn't sure what to do about her daughter's attitude.

"Well," Jason stood to his feet. "I think I will mosey on down the street for a bit. I feel like the mood in the room is shifting, and I'm not sure if the male species will be welcome much longer." He grimaced and Reesa offered him an apologetic and tired smile. He gave her a reassuring pat on the back as he leaned across the counter towards Jamie. She startled at his closeness, and he flashed one of his devastating smiles as he slid his fingers behind her ear. She felt him tuck something behind her curls. "Thanks for the cup of joe, Red, and the awesome company. Maybe you could send one of those muffins my way later. See you ladies around." He winked at them all as he grabbed Jamie's keys, unlocked the door, and departed. Reesa exhaled a loud breath as Jamie's keys dangled from the lock.

"Whoa. What was that about?" Reesa fanned herself as she pointed to Jamie's hair and walked over to grab the keys he'd left behind. "A little napkin flower for you, a sexy smile, and intentional eye contact... girl, what were you two up to?"

Jamie could feel the warmth creep up her neck and into her cheeks at the unusual attention. "I have no idea. We've just been chatting. He had only been here about fifteen minutes before you two came knocking. Besides, Jason's always been a flirt."

"I don't think I've ever seen him that ostentatious." Reesa glanced at her watch. "Theo should be getting to work soon. I'd love to see him."

"It's been like three hours, Mom..." Clare nagged. "He looks the same, I promise you."

"Alright, sour puss." Jamie swatted Clare's elbow with a towel, the loud pop and sting causing the girl to jump in her seat.

"Hey!" She rubbed her elbow.

"You need to be kind. I know you're tired. I know you're upset with Teddy, but none of us had anything to do with that, so you can take that frustration and channel it elsewhere, preferably into something productive instead of temper. Do I need to call Billy Lou?"

"Lord, no." Clare cringed at the idea of Billy Lou interfering with her funky mood.

"Then get it together. I want my upbeat and happy Clare back." Jamie walked over to the stereo she housed on the back counter and pressed the button, cranking the volume as a fast tempo blasted from the speakers. Clare instinctively covered her ears, as did Reesa, before Jamie started dancing behind the counter. Reesa joined in and both, with their over-the-top dance moves, slowly coaxed the girl out of her sour mood and into an emerging grin before she tiredly joined in on their shenanigans.

"Mornin', Theo." Jason lifted his cup of coffee in salute as Theo Whitley walked up to his garage office and whipped out his keys.

"You're awfully early." Theo opened the glass door and held it open as Jason walked inside and waited patiently as Theo turned on all the lights and fired up his computer. The smell of grease, floor cleaner, and a light scent of apple cinnamon lingered in the air.

"Had a busy morning. Just saw Reesa and Clare over at Jamie's."

Theo glanced up for more of an explanation and Jason sighed as he sat in one of the free chairs in the waiting area. "They look and feel about as tired as we do."

"Glad you found Teddy," Theo remarked, sitting in his own chair behind his desk.

"Poor kid is going to have a terrible next few days after getting the town so up in arms."

Theo shrugged. "Serves him right. Maybe he'll learn his lesson."

"I never did."

"He's not you," Theo replied, his quick retort stinging a bit. "You were the one to throw those stupid parties back in the day. Teddy was just a fool wanting to check it out."

"True. Though I never realized I had the reputation I did until Red called me last night. Quite impressed they'd choose my property."

"Gloating in your legacy?" Theo scoffed and shook his head as Jason laughed.

"Some legacy, huh? Hey, I'd much rather be known for that than for other mistakes I've made. We can't all be the honorable Theodore Whitley." Theo's typical glower only deepened. "Hey, don't get me wrong, I like you now, but boy did I hate you in high school. Secretly, of course." Jason toasted towards him with a sly smirk. "And you can't say the feelings weren't mutual."

Grunting, Theo agreed and typed a quick password into his computer to unlock the screen. "When did you want to get started this morning?"

"Whenever you're ready," Jason replied. "You're my only appointment until ten. I've got another call across town at Lee Hubbard's property. He wants a new barn."

"You able to take on two big projects at the same time?" Theo asked.

"Don't worry, yours is priority. But I need all the projects I can get to pay off Janessa."

"Would that be the first or second wife?" Theo quipped.

"Second." Jason took a melancholy sip of his coffee. "Women are expensive."

"Never had that problem."

"You'll understand soon enough." Jason tilted his head over his shoulder towards the coffee shop. "Reesa and Clare... I can only imagine two at once." He grimaced. "But really, they're not too bad in the beginning. It's the middle and the end when things go awry."

"For you," Theo clarified. "I don't intend to have that problem."

"Let's hope you don't. Again, it gets expensive."

"You still paying for the divorce?"

"Lord, no. I'm paying off her debts."

Confusion flashed across Theo's face and Jason sighed. "Never mind. It's my problem and my recompense. How about we get started with those measurements and plans?"

"Sounds good." Theo stood, his stature broader and stouter than Jason's but matched in comfortable heights above six feet tall. The small office felt even smaller with the two of them standing. Theo motioned out the garage door and opened the large bay doors on their way to the side of the building where he intended for Jason to build the new car wash.

"I think Jamie is onto your plans here," Jason informed him.

"I don't doubt it."

"When do you plan to tell Reesa?"

Theo smirked. "I don't. I'm letting her figure it out on her own."

"She's going to *love* you," Jason chuckled.

"Thankfully, she already does."

"But this is different. This is... a gesture, man. Like, *the* gesture. You're building this for her. And it's... big."

"Yeah," Theo replied.

BRUSHED BY HOPE

"Is this... I mean, I ask this with the friendliest intentions, because I know what this is going to mean to a woman. Is this what you want? I mean... this is game-changer level."

"I've wanted her from the moment I met her." His unshakable response and serious expression impressed Jason. Theo was always the clear-headed one of the two of them. Focused. Determined. Smart. Careful.

"Well, she is beautiful, I'll give you that. And funny." Theo's right brow quirked in his direction. "What? A man can't appreciate?"

"A man, yes. You? No."

"I'm offended." Jason held a hand to his heart with a smile. And though he played the insult off in jest, he also did feel its sting. His reputation was that of a careless and woman-hungry man. If only people knew how far off the mark that really was. But instead of defending himself, he played the part to keep life simple. Let people think what they want, and he will focus on himself for a bit. He had to work. He had to pay off debts that were not his own. And he had to heal. Because despite what others thought, he did have a heart and it had been broken, stomped on, and disappointed... two times.

"So, what's the plan?" Theo asked, nodding towards the blank slate of land in front of them.

"Well, I mapped out measurements for the most part. Will need to get an official survey of the place. I talked to Betty about that last week and have it lined up for next Tuesday. The geotechnical guys will be here Wednesday the following day. I took some soil samples and should have the results back this week, so they'll have those to go on too. I just want to make sure we are all on the same page with what building materials are best. Since you'll have a lot of water running through here and absorbing, I want us to make sure we have all our bases covered for a strong foundation."

"Didn't think about the geotechnical side." Theo rubbed his stubbled chin and nodded in approval.

"After that, we'll go over plans a final time to make sure that the soil results match what we are planning and then I can get to ordering materials. You want various bids on that? Or you want me to stick to Talley's?" He motioned up the street to the local lumberyard and Theo nodded.

"Stick to Talley's."

"They aren't always the best price," Jason warned.

"That's okay. I'd rather keep business local."

"Understood." Jason respected that response. He also knew that was one of the main reasons Theo asked him to do the job as well. There were other contractors and carpenters out there, but he was local, and Theo was nothing but loyal to Piney. Jason extended his hand and Theo shook it. "It's going to look pretty impressive."

"Let us hope." Theo turned at the sound of a loud whistle and his shoulders relaxed as he caught sight of Reesa walking in their direction.

Jason watched as her face split into an enamored smile as she slid into Theo's arms and wrapped hers around his waist. Her head rested comfortably against his chest a moment before she tilted her head back to gaze up at him. "I've needed that *all* morning. My teenager is kicking my butt today."

Theo's brow narrowed in concern. "How so?"

"Oh, she is in the worst mood. Just ask Jason." Reesa nodded towards him as she rested her cheek back against Theo in a comfortable hug. "She about chewed into him over at Jamie's."

Jason held up his finger. "I was smart and got out of there beforehand."

"That you were. Talk about reading the room." Reesa grinned. "He was an expert."

"I've had lots of practice," Jason chuckled as he rested his hands in his back pockets.

"What are you two doing out here?" Reesa asked, releasing her hold on Theo and staring at the plain parcel in front of them.

"Oh, looking at maybe adding a couple extra bays to the garage." Theo motioned over his shoulder to his shop and Reesa tilted her head as if envisioning his plan.

"Hmm..." She eyed Jason and he purposely avoided her gaze as he, too, looked out over the piece. "Okay." Reesa accepted the explanation, though her tone held a slight touch of disbelief. "Well, I am going to meet Billy Lou at the diner for a giant breakfast. She said Charlie is working off his morning of fraught nerves by burying his head in that truck for Clare he's been tinkering with, and she's fretted and worked up an appetite. So, I, being the sweet and understanding person that I am, volunteered to suffer through fluffy pancakes, crisp bacon, and fresh squeezed orange juice."

"Suffering becomes you," Jason complimented and had her laughing.

Theo lightly squeezed her hand. "Bring me a coffee afterwards, please."

"I will. A big one. I can tell you need it." She cupped his cheek in her hand and stood on her tiptoes a brief moment to plant a tender kiss to his lips. "You're a good man, Theo Whitley. And I like the look of you." She winked as she pulled away to walk up the sidewalk. "And you, Jason Wright, better be good today."

He tapped his temple in a farewell salute as she turned and wandered up the walk.

"Yep, you got a good one there." Jason turned to see Theo studying him in quiet, intense contemplation. He held up his hands in innocence. "No evil Reesa-stealing plan in my future. Just making an observation and appreciating the view," he defended. "Besides, you two fit. Nobody could interfere with the two of you." Tension released from Theo's face. "I'll be seeing you, Theo. I'll let you know the results of the soil test as soon as I get'em." Jasons shook Theo's hand one more time and then made his way towards his truck parked in front of Java Jamie's. He could feel fatigue setting in as he sat in his front seat and buckled his seat belt. He leaned his head back against the headrest and closed his eyes. One appointment down, one more to go, and then maybe he could catch a nap. A knock on his window had him cracking open one eye and turning his head to see Jamie standing on the other side of the glass. Her eyes gleamed with her genuine kindness. He rolled down his window and she smiled. "How are you still so chipper?" Jason asked.

She held up a large cup steaming with coffee. "Because I literally work around caffeine *all day*." She giggled and he couldn't help but smile at her bright, dancing blue eyes. She handed him the cup and he reached for some wadded up bills in his cup holder. "Don't worry about it. A hero's brew."

"Hero." He smirked. "Never gotten that before."

"Well, soak it up then. Also—" She handed a paper sack through the window as well. "Muffins. As promised."

"You're spoiling me, sweetheart." Jason rubbed a tired hand over his face as he accepted the treat. He noted a light pink flush stained her cheeks at his comment, and he wondered why that would make Jamie blush. "Thanks for this." He held up the bag and nodded towards the coffee cup that now resided in his cupholder.

"You're welcome. See you around." Jamie walked back into her shop, and he watched through the windows for a moment as she greeted another customer with energetic enthusiasm and a ready smile. The woman was a gem in Piney. No... she was a ruby, he decided, because of the bright red hair she sported. And like the rarest rubies, her transparency and genuine vibrancy made her even more valuable. Piney's hidden ruby. He smirked and wondered how Jamie would respond to such a description. He decided he'd soon like to find out.

CHAPTER THREE

The familiar cabin that once looked staged as one in a horror film beckoned Jamie with its bright pots of impatiens and petunias, a vibrant welcome mat, and various windchimes in various shapes and colors. Reesa Tate tended to leave her mark on just about anything she touched, and her vivid personality brought life to even the most tired of souls, including Billy Lou's abandoned cabin. The Tate women had been renting from Billy Lou since they came to town, and though Theo and Reesa grew more serious by the day in their relationship, the little cabin remained home for Reesa and Clare. The door opened and Trooper, Theo's dog, fled outside, stopping briefly with a few swishes of the tail to look at Jamie before he bounded through the woods to head to Theo's house. Clare stood at the doorway, holding it open for Jamie as she carried foil pans containing their supper. Billy Lou's sporty SUV was parked to the side of the cabin already and Jamie could just make out her familiar hoot of laughter from inside. "Gangs all here," Clare said with a smiled.

"Glad to see you in upbeat spirits finally." Jamie stepped over the threshold and paused a moment so her eyes adjusted.

"Well, it's about time." Billy Lou rushed towards her and removed the pans, her eyes quickly scanning the writing on top. "Three-fifty, Reesa. Get that oven hot." Billy Lou's eyes sparkled as she looked back to see Reesa hopping to her feet to do her bidding. "Welcome, sweetie. It's good to see you," she clucked, her attention back on Jamie as she walked the foil pans to the counter.

"Sorry I'm late. Took me a little longer to close up shop today."

"No worries." Reesa reached for a wine glass and filled a double portion of blush before handing it to Jamie. "I was just telling Billy Lou about Theo trying to pull a fast one on me." She rolled her eyes heavenward. "As if he could."

"What do you mean?" Jamie asked, attempting to tamper down her knowledge of such a subject.

"Oh, he and Jason Wright think they're *so* clever over at the garage."

"Fill me in," Jamie invited, accepting a cracker from Clare and dipping it into a cream cheese and chutney appetizer. The tangy combination made her dance in her chair. "Yum!"

"A Billy Lou concoction," Clare stated, taking her own heaping cracker and snacking. "Never a bad one."

Billy Lou smoothed a hand over Clare's ponytail in response. "Now, Reesa, just because he hasn't shared details on the project doesn't mean he's trying to pull a fast one."

"Don't give me that. You're in cahoots with them." Reesa pointed a finger at her, and Billy Lou chuckled. "See? She admits it."

"I admitted nothing," Billy Lou challenged. "I'm laughing because you are so sure of yourself."

"And why shouldn't I be? Theo denies anything suspicious every time I ask him about it. He won't even tell me what he's doing other than "a few extra bays." He doesn't need a few extra bays. Then he'd have to hire more mechanics, and I know he's not doing that because my daughter, the spy, works there, and she said he hasn't mentioned it."

Jamie eyed Clare curiously to see if the teen did indeed know nothing of Theo's plans. She looked blankly at the cream cheese and took another bite.

"And you..." Reesa pointed at Jamie. "All chummy with *Mr. Wright*. What's that about? Do you know something too?"

Jamie choked on her bite and waved her hands to clear up any confusion. "Jason and I have no secrets, trust me. He just came to the shop the one morning after finding Teddy. I haven't even seen him since."

The chime of the oven sounded, and Reesa paused in her rant to slip the foil pans inside and set the timer. "Thirty-five minutes?" she asked.

"That'll do it," Jamie replied. Reesa confirmed her time and then walked over to the table to sit amongst her friends. "Why don't you tell us what you think is going on."

Reesa narrowed her gaze at Jamie and studied her. "Alright... I'll oblige, but don't think I'm not still onto you."

Jamie giggled and wriggled her eyebrows to make Clare and Billy Lou grin.

"I don't think Theo is lying in the sense that he *is* adding onto his business. Obviously, the location gives that away," Reesa began. "But the area mapped off with survey flags is two times the size of his current garage bays. So why is that, you ask? Because it's not for bays, otherwise would he not make them the same size as the other ones?"

"What if he's wanting to work on larger vehicles? Like eighteen-wheelers?" Jamie suggested.

Reesa's face fell before she plonked her forehead to the table and moaned. "That makes so much sense it hurts."

Billy Lou guffawed. "Honey, what in the world did you think he was doing?"

"A carwash," Reesa admitted. "I thought he was trying to surprise me with a carwash. I should have known Theo would be too sensible to do that."

"Why would a carwash not be sensible?" Jamie asked. "I still think it's a good idea."

"Oh, he said he ran the numbers, and he didn't think it would be as big of a success as I thought it would." Reesa grumbled as she pushed her hair back from her face. "Oh well. I guess it's water hoses and dish soap from here on out, Clare."

Clare shook her head. "You're on your own now. I've got my own truck to wash."

"Not yet, you don't," Reesa whined.

"Mom, Mr. Charlie has me wiping it down every time I'm there. Even if we just pop the hood to take a look at his and Teddy's work. He says I have to put in the time when I can. Which, by the way, would be more if Teddy wasn't there all the time."
"Why don't you want to be around Teddy?" Jamie asked. "You still mad at him?"

"That would be a yes," Clare said. "He has yet to even reach out to me since prom night. He's avoided me at school, and he hasn't texted or called either."

"Have you messaged him?" Jamie asked.

"Yes. I blew up his phone the next day so I could check on him and he never replied. And I know for a fact he has his phone back because I saw him with it at school."

"Maybe he's just embarrassed." Reesa rubbed a hand on Clare's back. "Or he knows you're upset with him."

"How would he know that? He hasn't spoken to me."

"Could be the red face and smoke comin' out of your ears," Billy Lou smirked. "Honey, he'll come around. Y'all are too good of friends for him not to. Just be kind when he does. Friendship is more important than being right."

"Right about what?" Jamie asked.

Clare sighed heavily and plopped her cheek into her hand, the gesture so like her mother's Jamie had to smile. "I've really been struggling with the whole 'I told you so' mindset when it comes to all this. I'm trying not to be like that, but it's hard. I told him not to go to that stupid party and he went anyway. And what happens? It gets busted by the cops, his new 'friends' abandon him, so he flees on foot and has to sleep in a chicken coop all night, and then he is grounded for like a month. If he had just listened to me, he wouldn't be in this situation, and we would still be friends. But no. He didn't listen, and now he's still hanging out with his new 'friends,' and they don't care about him, otherwise they would not have left him that night. But he just doesn't see it. So yeah... I'm kind of struggling."

"We all are," Reesa admitted. "But sometimes kids just have to learn their lessons the hard way."

"That's what Mr. Charlie says," Clare explained. "He said he did his fair share of stupid things in high school, and he eventually learned, but it took him forever. I don't want Teddy to be an old man before he wises up."

Billy Lou roared in laughter as she slapped her thigh. "Oh, this is too good. Sweetie, Charlie Edwards learned his lesson long before he returned to Piney. Have hope for Teddy. I have a feeling he will come around." She squeezed Clare's knee as she hopped to her feet to check the supper.

"Show grace to get grace," Reesa reminded her daughter. "How many times have I screwed up over the years?" Reesa nudged Clare's shoulder until she responded.
"A lot."

"And how many times did you forgive me?"

"Every time."

"Exactly. And how many times have you screwed up over the years?"

"A lot," Clare admitted.

"And how many times have I forgiven you?"

"I get it."

"Answer the question," Reesa continued.

"Every time," Clare muttered.

"Exactly. *Every* time. Because my relationship with you is more important than whether or not I'm right all the time. Show Teddy some grace. He made a bad choice; you make them too. It's not fair to hold it over his head."

"Even if I planned to forget all about it, he wouldn't know because he won't talk to me." Clare took a sip of her tea, her eyes growing glassy. "I think I'm going to take this to my room for now." She stood and hurried down the hall.

"Bless her heart." Billy Lou shook her head.

"Hard-headed people are the worst," Reesa sighed and then blanched at the pointed stares from Jamie and Billy Lou. "What?"

"You are one of the hardest heads in Piney, girl," Jamie laughed.

"I guess you're kind of right... second only to Billy Lou."

Billy Lou bit back a smile as she tried to remain sober. "I prefer resolute."

"Oooooo I like that." Jamie fisted her hands on her hips. "Resolute. Yep, I'm going to steal that."

"There is a stubbornness about me that never can bear to be frightened at the will of others," Reesa sighed, and Jamie giggled at Billy Lou's confused face.

"A quote," Jamie explained. "She's always got one from a book or movie bumping around in that head of hers."

"Pride and Prejudice," Reesa explained and then gasped that Billy Lou didn't recognize it. "Elizabeth Bennet… only *the* most stubborn and proud character ever written in literature, Billy Lou; aside from Mr. Darcy, of course. And one of the best love stories *ever*."

"Please tell me you've forced Theo to watch Pride and Prejudice." Jamie grinned as Reesa nodded. "I bet he loved that."

"He didn't last through the whole thing. In fact, I believe his exact words were, "This about done? I've got a life to live." The women all laughed at the predictable response when Jamie's phone buzzed on the table. Jason Wright's name popped up on the screen and Reesa's brows lifted. "Well, well, well! Mr. Wright is calling… again."

"Oh, it's probably nothing." Jamie waved her hand at her phone and ignored the call. "I'm with you guys, he can leave a voicemail." Not long after the ringing had ended, a voicemail chimed, immediately followed by a text. Concern had Jamie's brow furrowing as she looked down at her phone. "Okay, this isn't normal, so I'm going to check this." She stood up to allow herself some privacy in the living room as she listened to Jason's voicemail. She overheard Reesa telling Billy Lou about the other morning in the coffee shop and how Jason had been hanging around and flirting. It wasn't new behavior for him. She wished it meant something more than just his usual tendencies, but it didn't. Jason Wright had always been and probably would always be a massive flirt. Jamie was just his latest target because he needed coffee in the mornings. But despite reminding herself of his behavior, her heart still did thump a little faster when his deep voice spoke into her ear.

"Hey Red, it's Jason. I've got a favor to ask you, so when you get a chance, shoot me a call or message. Nothing serious, just need to run something by you. I hope you're out getting into some shenanigans. Have fun." He hung up and Jamie then looked down to read the text message he'd sent her. Same thing, nothing to elaborate on what he needed, and curiosity got the best of her. She dialed him back and he answered on the first ring. "That was quick."

"Well, it seemed urgent— a call *and* a text. What's up?"

"Not urgent. I'm just a fool."

"Tell me something I don't know," she teased. "Now, what can I do for you, Jason?"

He chuckled on the other end and the rumbling sound sent butterflies dancing inside her stomach. He had a great voice, she realized; a great laugh, an easy charm that rolled off him in lazy waves. "I've overbooked my crew this week, starting tomorrow."

"Okay..."

"Well," He sighed into the line. "When I do that, I always feel bad because they work overtime and what not. Anyway, I'd like to feed them each day this week, so I was going to see if I could order some boxes of breakfast sandwiches for the crew and then maybe a giant supply of coffee over the next few days?"

"How many people?" Jamie asked.

"About fifteen of us."

"How many days?"

"The rest of this week, so four days."

"Starting tomorrow morning?"

"Yes ma'am."

"What time did you want to pick up in the mornings?"

"We get started early. What time will you have it available? I can always send someone over to grab it all."

"What time do you need it, Jason?" she repeated.

"We start at five."

"I'll have it ready at 4:45. Breakfast sandwiches... probably some high protein combinations, some muffins just for something sweet, and maybe—" She paused. "I'll get something together for you."

"Red, you're the best. Are you sure it's not too big of an ask? I know it's sort of late notice and a big order for so early."

"It's nothing new for me," she assured him. "Though tips are highly appreciated," she sang in a jingle to make him laugh and she was rewarded with his deep rumble.

"I'll make sure you are. Thanks, Jamie."

"You're welcome. See you in the morning." She hung up and turned to find Reesa and Billy Lou staring at her.

"She just overcommitted herself to a handsome face," Billy Lou murmured to Reesa.

"Elementary, my dear Watson. Elementary." Reesa imitated a British accent as she steepled her fingers and studied Jamie.

"Oh, stop that." Jamie waved away her scrutiny and walked back to the table. "He was ordering food for his work crew."

"He could have chosen the diner," Reesa pointed out.

"Or donuts from that little food truck on Price Street," Billy Lou suggested.

"But I'm the best in town." Jamie fisted her hands on her hips. "And don't you be getting donuts at that food truck, Billy Lou Whitley, or you'll hurt my feelings."

Laughing, Billy Lou waved away her concern. "Honey, the last time these hips saw a donut was in 1968. Now, Charlie on the other hand... I've seen evidence in his truck of his cheating on you. But not too much. I've been making him watch his sugar intake, so he's been better."

Jamie gasped. "Charlie Edwards..." She shook her head. "I'm going to make him add a dollar to the tip jar next time he comes in for recompense."

Reesa's lips quirked into a grin. "Really though, Jason does seem to be more present these days."

"I don't know what to tell you. Maybe because he's in town more now that he's working with Theo." She held up her hands and then went back to snacking on crackers and cheese. "I'll take the extra business though. Never hurts."

"Spoken like a true businesswoman." Billy Lou complimented, her attention shifting to her purse as her cell phone buzzed. She reached in and swiped with her red-tipped finger. "Charlie Edwards, what are you doin' callin' me? I'm with my girls." She rolled her eyes as she stood and walked towards the living room. "Well, I don't know what to tell you. You know this is my night at the cabin... Oh, alright. Let yourself in and there's some leftover chicken salad in the refrigerator. I've got that loaf of sourdough bread on the counter... Yes, the one from Betty... Help yourself. I'll be home by eight so we can watch the news." She air-kissed into the phone and then hung up. "Helpless, I tell ya."

"But you love it." Reesa winked at her, and Billy Lou's cheeks flushed.

"You know, I really do. Feels nice having a man's presence around the house again, even if he does just buzz in for meals and tv. Oh, and to bring

Sugar over. That little puppy has just won my heart. I hate to admit it."

"Have y'all talked about... oh, I don't know, the 'm' word?" Jamie asked curiously.

"Marriage?" Billy Lou smiled. "We have, but we just don't want to rush things. Though I'd be lying if I said I hadn't thought about it a lot over the last several months. He's about done workin' on that house and keeps saying he's moving into an apartment in town, but I just can't fathom that. He would hate living in an apartment."

"And you want him to live with you?" Reesa asked.

"The thought has crossed my mind, but only if we're married. I don't know how he feels about the idea yet. The moving in part, that is. I mean, it was the house I shared with Jerry. I don't know if Charlie would feel weird about that or if it even matters to him."

"It's changed a lot since Jerry passed, Billy Lou. You've done a lot to that place. I doubt it would feel weird to Charlie," Jamie encouraged.

"Time will tell. Lord knows I'm in no hurry."

Clare walked back into the kitchen and plopped in her empty seat. "Is the food ready yet?"

"Oh yes, teenager, it is." Billy Lou clucked over to the oven and worked with diligent hands to dish up plates for everyone. "Are you in better humor?"

Clare nodded, though her chin rested in her hand on the table.

"Good."

"Grandpa texted me," Clare reported to Reesa. "He wanted to see if we were free on Saturday; he thought he'd come up from Hot Springs and spend the day."

"Well, that is lovely." Billy Lou smiled. "I'm so glad Roger is making such an effort. Have you enjoyed getting to know him, Clare?"

Clare perked up in her seat and her shoulders relaxed. "I have. I like him."

Reesa smiled at her daughter as she continued to fill Billy Lou and Jamie in on her last visit with Roger Tate. "He said Grandma still isn't quite sure she wants to connect, but..." Clare shrugged her shoulders. "I'm starting to be okay with that. At first, it made me mad, but then I remind myself that I'm awesome and mom's awesome, and it's just her loss."

"That it is." Jamie toasted towards Clare. "And our gain."

"Most definitely," Billy Lou echoed. "And Theodore's gain. My, how you two have just opened up his world! I will forever be indebted to you for that. To see him so happy just warms me up from my French twist to my painted toenails."

Giggling at Billy Lou's expression, Jamie let her mind drift to her morning workload and what she planned to make for Jason and his crew. Jason enjoyed her cranberry and orange zest muffins. Whenever he ventured into the shop and bought a treat, that was what he chose. So she made a mental note to make a couple of those just for him. She listened to her friends chatter on about Clare's latest school ventures, the year soon coming to a close and how she planned to work more at Theo's garage and on her vintage truck with Charlie over the summer. Good topics, good friends, and good food— three of Jamie's favorite things in life— but her mind kept wandering to a handsome face and charming smile that she couldn't wait to see in the morning. It was foolish, she knew, to hope for more than a passing glance from Jason Wright, but she also enjoyed this newly introduced level of friendship they'd recently started. And if that was all that ever came to pass between them, she'd admire him from a distance just like she always had and enjoy having him as a friend. But she had to admit that she also couldn't help that slight twinge of longing when she thought about his bright eyes and sexy smile. Soured at her own ridiculous line of thought, Jamie finished off her meal and began clean-up duty in the kitchen before making her excuses to head back to her loft above her shop. She had an early morning, and she was going to make sure she was ready when Jason Wright rolled up. Ready and waiting.

^

It was half past four in the morning and Jason pulled into the front parking spot outside Java Jamie's. The lights were out, and he saw no movement inside. She agreed to prepare breakfast for his crew. He ran through their phone conversation and there was no doubt in his mind they'd agreed, but where was she? He glanced up to the second story and saw a faint light shining behind the heavy blinds and curtains. Her loft. He climbed out of his truck and walked around to the back of the building, Jamie's car parked under a small metal covering proved she was home. He climbed the old metal staircase, the steps shifting beneath his work boots making him a bit nervous as he continued up. He reached a small wooden threshold that had just enough room for one potted plant and a welcome mat. A cheerful sign on the door read: "No admittance except on party business." A Lord of the Rings reference that told him it had been a gift from Reesa. He raised his hand and knocked. The quiet street below and the still air allowed him to hear the shuffling from within the small loft apartment. The porch light flicked on and then the locks turned.

Jamie swung the door open, her bright and cheerful smile greeting him. "You beat me."

"I was a bit nervous you'd forgotten." Jason smiled and pointed to her door. "I apologize for coming to your house and knocking. I saw the light on—"

"It's all good. I would normally be down in the shop, but I was dragging this morning after weekly girls' night and just decided to bake everything up here."

"Girls' night, hm?" He leaned against the door jamb as she bustled around her tiny apartment. It was cramped but tidy, and bright colors adorned most of the walls and furniture. It fit Jamie's personality perfectly.

"Yep," she continued. "Reesa, Billy Lou, Clare, and I get together every Monday evening for dinner at Reesa's cabin. It sort of just became a thing, and now none of us miss it."

"Well, that's cool." Jason continued to study the interior, intrigued to see the personal side of Jamie.

"Come on in and shut the door. You're letting all the bought air out." Jamie waved him inside. "I'm just boxing up the rest of it. Won't be long."

The efficiency layout gave him full view of Jamie's entire house as he walked towards her small island that separated the kitchen from her living area. "How long have you lived above the shop?"

"Since I bought it... so a long time, I guess." She looked up and smiled, pausing a moment to watch him looking around. He flushed at being discovered and focused on her boxing up several wrapped breakfast sandwiches and placing them in heating bags. "I found these delivery bags in my old food truck supplies. Man, am I glad to not have to work in a small truck anymore. But I kept some of my supplies. Turns out these will be quite handy for you the next few days in keeping everything warm."

The quantity and variety of food astonished him and Jamie never broke stride as she talked, stuffing sandwich after sandwich into the warming bag. "How long have you been up?" Jason asked.

"Since about three."

"*Three?*" Jason shook his head. "Jamie, why didn't you tell me you would have to get up so early to do this?"

"It's not that early for me. I typically get up at 3:30 or 4 anyway, so an extra thirty minutes was no big deal. Besides, I keep the good stuff up here." She motioned towards her coffee pot and then blanched. "I'm sorry, I didn't offer you a cup."

He held up his hand and motioned to the work in front of her. "I think you're okay. You've gone above and beyond." Her red curls were tied back into her usually messy bun on top of her head, but a few ringlets framed her face. She tied a bright handkerchief as a headband, and he thought he detected a light touch of makeup around her eyes. "You have big plans today at the shop?"

"No, just the usual. Though it is Tuesday; I usually have a couple of women's groups come in and chat together." She zipped the warming bag and nudged it towards him. "There's bag number one and here is bag number two." She slid a small paper sack across the counter. "That is for you."

"Oh really?" His brows perked a bit as he opened the small bag and peeked inside. The sweet and tangy smell of his favorite muffins wafted up to him. "Ooooh man." Jason beamed, impressed that she remembered his choice of muffin and touched that she'd make him his own special batch. "You didn't have to do this."

She grinned as she grabbed a separate container of the muffins. "These are for the shop. Two birds, one stone. You haven't bought one in a while, so I thought it would be a fun surprise. Mind helping me carry some things down? I mean, I might as well put you to work while you're here." She chuckled to herself as she stacked several containers for him to carry, then grabbed a load herself and headed out the front door. He followed obediently. "You need to lock up?"

"Nah, I don't usually worry about it." She navigated the creaky staircase like a professional and unlocked the back door to the coffee shop. She flicked light switches with her elbow as they walked into the small back room full of stock. "Just follow me, Mr. Wright." She hustled across the small space, through swinging doors and out to behind her work counter.

"I've never been on this side of the bar." He studied all the mixes, ingredients, syrups, sauces, and dishes, everything organized, clean, and crowded. "Everything seems to have its place."

"Yep. That's the way I like it." She removed the apron she wore and grabbed a fresh one from a hook. "All I have to do is get your coffee going. I have carafes in that cupboard over there if you don't mind grabbing me two of them."

"Not at all." He walked over to a large wooden wardrobe and opened the doors. He spotted the carafes and set them on the counter. "Anything else?"

"Just grab two to-go cups there." She motioned with her head towards the large paper cups near the register and he obediently fetched two of them. She scooped, mixed, flavored, and pressed button after button until the incredible smell of coffee began flooding the room. She then set to work creating concoctions for the two cups, and he noticed one of them was his usual drink of choice. She finished it, placed a lid on top, and handed it to him, while taking a sip of her own on her way back towards the carafes. The woman never stopped moving, her hands constantly in motion, completing task after task. "

You're a wonder, Red."

Jamie paused in transferring coffee into a carafe and looked up. "Why's that?"

"You're like the Energizer Bunny around here. I'm barely awake and trying to muster up the energy for the day's work and you've tackled more in two hours than I could in half a day."

She laughed, but a light pink tinged her cheeks. "It's easy when you love what you do. It's one of my biggest joys to wake up and run my own coffee shop. It's what I always wanted. So I try to tackle each day with more enthusiasm than the last."

"Well, if you ever want a job in construction, I'd hire you in a heartbeat. I don't think I've ever seen a person work so hard."

"Oh, I doubt that. There are plenty who are much more successful than me." Jamie looked away from him a moment and back to her work and he knew she meant his first ex-wife. Everyone thought him a fool for letting Cari go. The successful model and blooming actress. The girl who wanted it all... and then some. Sure, she'd been beautiful, gorgeous even, but all Cari had wanted was to leave Piney and make something of herself. To be adored. To be the center of someone's world. And Jason tried. He honestly had. They were young when they married; trying to figure out life, work, and marriage while also just branching out into the workforce was a challenge both of them struggled with. She wanted lights, cameras, and action out in California. He wanted to work with his hands and build a life in Piney. Neither had been mature enough to realize those two plans weren't compatible until they'd said "I do." They'd fought constantly. She'd cry and he would travel with her to audition after audition, to modeling job after modeling job until she finally landed a recurring spread for a clothing magazine. He had thought that would be enough for her. She'd have her pictures taken, have proof that she'd been glamorous and beautiful in a magazine, and then she'd settle back into life in Piney. He'd been wrong. Cari wanted more and he was holding her back. He'd attempted to support her. He moved to California, worked on various construction crews around the state while she networked in Hollywood. It didn't take long for her to win the attention she craved. She booked her first role in a daytime soap opera and instead of celebrating with a nice dinner and drinks, she handed him a manila envelope with divorce papers. He was baggage. He didn't dream big enough. He wasn't cut out for the new life she'd created. He was an embarrassment. And he signed those dreadful papers. He remembered her cheer of relief when he did so without argument. She'd clapped and hugged him and thanked him for 'setting her free,' but he still remembered the stab of pain her glee had wedged into his heart. He spent years looking for someone who not only wanted him but needed him too. Looking back now, he realized it wasn't exactly the healthiest approach, because then that led to issues in his second marriage. Another failure that he carried on his shoulders.

"Jason?" Jamie snapped in front of his face. "You okay?" Her concerned blue eyes studied his face. She briefly held the back of her palm to his forehead. "You look a little pale. Want to sit down a minute?"

He shook his head. "No, no... I'm fine. Sorry, I just... got lost in thought for a second. Completely fine." He forced a smile and took a sip of his coffee and then held up his cup. "I just need more of this and then I'll be golden."

He could tell she wasn't fully convinced, but she was too busy preparing his order to hover over him. She glanced at the clock on the wall and squealed, speeding up in her movements until she placed the last carafe on the counter. "Done! 4:45! Phew!" Smiling proudly, she waved at the warming bags, stacked boxes, and the full carafes. "Your order, Mr. Wright, is complete and on time."

He couldn't help but smile as she danced her signature jig before grabbing an armload and walking towards the front entrance. "I'll help you load up."

"Jamie, you're going to wear yourself out before opening time if you don't slow down a bit." He caught up as she was finagling her keys in the door lock to unlock the extra bolts she'd installed. *Probably herself*, he thought. He gripped the back of her hand as she attempted to turn the key without dropping her armful of boxes. She stiffened at his touch and quickly slipped her hand back to her boxes as he turned the key in the lock. He opened the door and held it open so she could pass through first, and then opened his passenger door to set the warming bag in his seat. She placed the boxes on top of it. "Where should I put the coffee?"

"Probably the floor board. Though I would still drive slow. They shouldn't leak or spill, but better safe than sorry." She bustled away to fetch one and he hurried after her. They placed them in his truck and she swiped her hands on a dish towel that was slung over her shoulder. "Alright, you're all set. I hope your crew enjoys them all. Make sure you tell them where you got it." She winked and playfully fluffed her bun.

"Of course."

She waved and hurried back inside her shop. She didn't lock up behind herself and he made his way back through the door, the jingle of the bell causing her to turn and look his direction. "Did we forget something?" She began looking around and then palmed her forehead before grabbing a stack of napkins and shoving them his direction. "Sorry about that."

"No," he chuckled. "Take a breath, Red."

She did, a deep inhale and exhale that he knew would probably be one of the few she would take time for during the day. "I need to pay you."

"Oh." She chuckled, embarrassed. "Well, I don't have the register opened up yet. So why don't we just settle at the end of the week?"

His brows lifted. "End of the week? How about at end of day? I don't want to throw off your bookkeeping or anything. And I can swing by here after quitting time and take care of it."

She placed her hands on her ample hips, her curves accentuated by the black apron cinched around her waist. He wasn't sure he'd ever noticed the subtle hourglass figure she sported; granted, he'd never taken the time to look. "It's whatever you want to do." Her words interrupted his thoughts. "I'll be here." She smiled. "And I don't plan on going anywhere."

"It's a date, then." Jason winked. "I'll swing by this afternoon and cash out. Maybe we can plan for tomorrow's order then, too."

"Okay." She nodded in agreement as she swiped her towel over her counter and rearranged her stack of napkins.

"Thanks again for this, Jamie. I appreciate it."

She motioned towards her clock. "I love when people want to talk sweet to me, but you're pushing your time, Jason." She grinned as he jolted into motion and walked back towards the door.

"See ya, Ruby Red." He flashed her one last smile as he motioned towards the lock on her door and she walked towards him, locking the deadbolt back into place. He nodded in approval and she shot him a thumbs up and appreciative smile before turning and walking back to her work counter. Her hands flew into action and he stood a moment watching her continue in her morning zeal of motion before remembering his bag of muffins that awaited him in his truck. He hopped inside to the smells of Java Jamie's, and he breathed deeply the entire drive over to his worksite.

CHAPTER FOUR

The morning never slowed down. Jamie prepared order after order as the morning waned on, grateful for the business, but also the extra pastries she'd prepared early that morning. By noon, she was worn out. By four, she was struggling to put one foot in front of the other. Thankfully a reprieve came. She now only had two customers in the shop: one reading quietly in a comfy chair and the other typing soundlessly on a laptop and drinking his second Earl Grey. The bell above the door jingled and she glanced quickly over her shoulder before swinging around to take a full double-take of the woman walking inside. As she lived and breathed, she could have sworn it was Reesa, but as the woman stepped closer into the room wearing a smart, white pant suit and sandals and an uncertain expression on her face,

Jamie could see the soft wrinkles around the eyes and mouth. This was Reesa's mother. She felt her stomach tighten, but she flashed a welcoming smile. "Hi there! Welcome to Java Jamie. I'm Jamie." She waved a hand over her messy apron. "I apologize for my wardrobe. I had a mishap topping off a frappuccino a bit ago. What can I get ya?"

The woman's eyes roamed over the menu board. "What is The Riddler?"

"Oh," Jamie beamed. "That's where I come up with a riddle of the day. If you guess the answer, you get your drink of choice for free."

"Ah." The woman briefly smiled and then waved away the opportunity. "I think I will do a cappuccino, please."

"Sure thing." Jamie began preparing the espresso as the woman stepped to the side and studied the décor of the shop. Did Reesa know her mother was in town? Was Reesa planning on meeting up with her? She hadn't texted Jamie about a meet up, and she would have... Well, she assumed Reesa would have. Because Reesa would be freaking out over it and would need someone to talk to. *Or...* Reesa didn't know Virginia Tate was in Piney. But why would she be if she hadn't contacted Reesa to meet up? And there was no doubt in Jamie's mind this was Virginia Tate, Reesa's mother, because the women looked exactly the same only a couple of decades apart in age. Did she contact Theo? Did she message him to see if Reesa had plans to meet up with her mother just in case Reesa didn't know Virginia was in town? She didn't want to cause any disturbance for Reesa if she didn't know. She fretted as she steamed the milk for the cappuccino and nervously glanced at the door as the bell jingled once more. Her heart dropped when she spotted Clare bouncing in, all smiles.

"Hey, Jamie. I was hoping to sweet-talk you into a coffee for Theo and a passion lemonade for me." She clasped her hands together and feigned a begging stature, much like her mother did on occasion. Jamie smiled.

"Of course. Give me one second with this." She hurriedly placed the cup on a saucer and walked it over to the far end of the counter. "Here you are." She warmly thanked Virginia Tate and watched as she walked over to a seat by the front windows and looked out the glass as she sipped.

Jamie then turned to see Clare leaning on the counter and peeking under the glass cookie display. "Oatmeal chocolate chip?"

"I'll give you two of those too." Jamie quickly made Clare's order while keeping a close eye on her estranged grandmother across the shop. "You finally talk with Teddy?"

"Nope. He's officially avoiding me. He won't return my calls, texts, or notes in his locker; so I've given up."

"Oh," Jamie's face fell. "I'm so sorry, Clare."

The teen shrugged but the hurt was evident in her eyes. "I mean, I get it. He wants to fit in with the cool crowd. And having an epic story from the party night has helped him do that. He's soaking it up, I guess. He has a new girlfriend and everything, which naturally is a girl that does not like me. So that might be why he's being distant too. His girlfriends never like me."

"Their loss."

"I know, right?" Clare smirked as she sipped her lemonade and watched Jamie bag up three cookies. "Mr. Charlie said he's stopped coming around to work on my truck, too, so it looks like Teddy Graham has decided not to be my friend anymore."

"I doubt that. He'll come to his senses. You two have been inseparable all year. I don't see how he can just drop you so quickly. Maybe when he comes up for air, he'll see how wonderful your friendship was and is and will come to."

"Billy Lou says the same thing, but I'm not quite convinced. Besides, if he's just going to drop me every time a pretty girl wants to cozy up with him, is he really that good of a friend? I mean, I thought we were best friends, but I guess I was wrong. Mom says not to let it get to me. And I'm trying not to let it. Theo... well, he wants to ring Teddy by the neck, so I try not to complain too much when I'm around him."

Jamie handed Clare the cookies, having slipped an extra one inside for her. "Well, I think you're great, and I'll be your friend no matter what."

"Thanks." Clare turned and paused, turning slowly back towards Jamie with wide eyes. "Does that woman look like Mom, or is it just me?"

Jamie tried to hide her awareness of the woman by rubbing a towel over the counter.

"Jamie," Clare hissed. "Is that my grandmother?"

"I believe so," she whispered back. "She paid cash, though, so I don't know for certain."

"Um, she's my mom's older twin, how could it not be?" Clare subtly turned again to take a better look. "Wow, she's so pretty," she whispered, almost in awe. "Is she meeting up with Mom?"

"I have no idea. I hated to text your mom and ask if she didn't know about her being in town."

Clare straightened her shoulders. "Well, either way, she's here, right? Might as well introduce myself."

"Clare, I wouldn't do—" Jamie's words drifted off into the air as the determined teen walked towards the older woman by the window.

"Hi." Clare approached and sat across from the woman. "Welcome to Piney."

Surprise lit the woman's face as she briefly turned her face towards Jamie as if seeking an explanation for a random teenager approaching her table. Her eyes drifted back to Clare. "Hello."

"Are you Virginia Tate?"

"I am," the woman stated curiously.

"Well, my name is Clare. And I'm your granddaughter."

Virginia Tate choked on her sip, but recovered quickly by pressing a napkin to her perfectly painted lips. She stared at Clare with wide eyes as Clare pulled the chair out across from her and sat. She reached into the small bag Jamie had given her and removed two cookies, placing one in front of her grandmother. "I have about ten minutes before I have to be at work, so why don't you tell me what brings you to Piney?"

Impressed by her gumption, Jamie sent a swift text to Theo claiming she needed Clare's help for a few minutes, and she might run late to the garage. She still wasn't sure if she should text Reesa. Watching like a hawk, Jamie attempted to appear nonchalant as she worked.

"It's lovely to meet you, Clare. I didn't recognize you. I've only ever seen a picture. Once." Virginia's smooth tone covered any traces of surprise as she nodded towards the cookie. "Thank you for this." She avoided Clare's direct gaze, the young girl soaking in the woman in front of her.

"So, why are you in Piney? Does Mom know you're here?" Clare asked pointedly. "She didn't mention it, that's why I'm asking. Though she probably wouldn't, on account of worrying about me and how I would feel about it."

"Oh, well, no... your mother does not know I am here."

"Okay..." Clare waved for her to continue, and Jamie wanted to laugh at how uncomfortable the older woman felt in front of Clare's boldness.

"I was passing through and thought— Well, I don't know what I thought. So, I paused to have a cup of coffee and to observe the little town."

"Grandpa's coming to see me on Saturday. Did he tell you?"

"He did. Yes."

"And you weren't going to come."

"I was not," Virginia answered respectfully.

"Why not? I mean, are you still mad at Mom?"

Sighing, Virginia set her cup down on its saucer. "There's more to it than that, I'm afraid."

"Okay. Let me text my boss really quick that I'm going to be late. I want to hear what could possibly keep you from coming to see Mom and me, and I have a feeling it's going to take more than ten minutes. It's okay, though. He won't mind. He's my mom's boyfriend, Theodore Whitley." She pointed up the street to the mechanic shop. "He's a pretty understanding guy, especially when it comes to family stuff." She whipped out her phone and Virginia shifted in her seat, completely unprepared to handle the escalating situation.

Jamie was proud of Clare. The teen wasn't being rude. Pushy, yes. Rude, not yet. And she had every right to be rude to the woman. More so, the eagerness for connection made Jamie's heart ache for the girl. She wanted so badly for her mother and grandmother to forgive one another and reconnect. Clare set her phone aside and a quick buzz in reply told Jamie Theo would be marching over any minute in protector mode.

"I think I've bought myself about five minutes before Theo comes to check on me." Clare was honest about that too, and Jamie shook her head in admiration at the girl. "You look like her, you know. You and Mom... you look a lot alike."

"I was surprised by that too when I last saw her," Virginia admitted. "And you're a beautiful young woman yourself."

"Thanks. I had prom this past weekend. My first prom to ever go to. It was okay, kind of boring, but I enjoyed dressing up. My dress was gorgeous, and Mom did my makeup for me." Virginia smiled softly, the topic one Jamie could tell she longed to listen to but didn't know how to interact with her long-lost granddaughter or if she even deserved the opportunity. "Listen, Grandma—" Clare paused. "I can call you, Grandma, can't I?"

Virginia's lips parted and a soft sob escaped before she recovered and nodded, tears welling up in her eyes.

"Okay, cool." Clare continued, reaching across the table and taking one of Virginia's hands. "Grandpa is coming Saturday to visit and hang out. You should come too. I've liked getting to know

Grandpa, and I would like to get to know you as well. I know you and Mom have issues. Trust me, *I know*," she stressed. "But I'm going to pull my teenager card here. I'm not allowed to use it very often; Mom doesn't let me. But in this scenario, I think I have a right to." Clare squeezed Virginia's hand. "It's not about you or Mom right now. It's about me. And I'm asking you to come."

"You are so darlin'." Virginia dabbed her eyes with her free hand. "Your mother would be appalled even knowing you're speaking to me right now. I wouldn't want to upset her."

Clare waved away her reply like it was a pesky fly. "No. No, she wouldn't. If you only knew how much she wanted to see you again..." Clare clamped her mouth shut. "Anyway, just tell me you'll think about it, please. I won't be upset if this weekend is too soon. I realize I've thrown you a curveball today. But please know that I would love a chance to get to know you and for you to know me. At the end of the day, we're family. And living in Piney has shown me that nothing on this earth is more important than family."

Virginia nodded. "Aren't you just a spectacular young woman?" Her watery smile blossomed as Clare stood to her feet.

"Jamie's oatmeal chocolate chip cookies are my favorite." Clare nodded to the cookie she'd placed in front of her grandmother and stared at the woman a moment longer. "It was nice to meet you, Grandma." She stood and pushed in her chair, grabbed her two drinks and extra cookies, and walked out of the shop. Theo intercepted her on the sidewalk, his worried and concerned face evident as he threw a protective arm over the girl's shoulder and walked with her the rest of the way to his garage. Jamie released a quiet, long, unsteady breath as she watched Virginia Tate quietly cry into her napkin as she watched Theo and Clare walk away. Now Jamie would text Reesa.

^

She'd propped her feet up just as a knock on the door sounded. Jamie mustered the energy to rise to her sore feet and shuffle towards the door. She opened to find Jason Wright standing on the patio. Again. He flashed his devilishly handsome smile as he leaned inward and pretended to remove a flower from behind her ear. The cute magic trick brought a smile to her face. "Okay, I forgive you for being late." She waved him inside and he laughed.

"Yes, I am. Sorry, Red. We were just in the swing of things and I wanted to wrap up where we were at before tomorrow. It kept us a little later than planned. But I'm here to pay up, so what do I owe you for this morning's grub?"

She handed him an invoice and he briefly glanced at it while grabbing his wallet out of his back pocket. He thumbed through cash and placed a wad on her table, along with the invoice. She didn't glance at it as she walked back to her couch and sank into its comfortable cushions on an exhausted sigh.

"Long day?"

"You could say that."
"Look, if you aren't up for whipping up breakfast for my crew tomorrow, that's perfectly okay."

"Oh, no. I'll be fine. It was just a *long* day. Physically and emotionally."

Concern had him easing onto the couch next to her. "Everything okay?"

She nodded. "Just a weird afternoon. I'll recover."

He narrowed his eyes on her face. "You'd tell me if something were wrong, wouldn't you?"

A smile tilted the corners of her lips and she sighed. "Probably not, but in this case, I am genuinely fine. I just had some interesting customers today that required extra energy and effort."

"Ah. Gotcha."

"How was your day?"

Surprised by the question, Jason relaxed against a floral throw pillow and crossed his ankle over his knee. "Well, it went pretty well. Productive, which is always a good sign on the first day of a new job."

"Good." Jamie shifted to climb to her feet as a timer rang out above her oven. He watched as she donned an oven mitt, reached into the hot oven, and withdrew a glass baking dish. The smells emanating across the apartment had his stomach audibly growling. Her head turned and her eyes widened before she laughed. "Goodness."

He placed a hand over his stomach and grimaced. "Yeah, sorry about that. No lunch and I have a talkative stomach when it gets angry at me."

"You haven't eaten since this morning?" Jamie asked.

He shrugged his shoulders as she rolled her eyes. "Come on, then." She motioned him towards her island as she withdrew two plates from her cupboard. She motioned to the dish. "It's just some chicken and vegetables, but I have some fresh bread over here too." She grabbed the loaf and opened its wrapping. He took two thick slices.

"You're going to spoil me, Red. Two meals in one day."

"Well, you shouldn't go all day without eating, Jason. Especially working in the heat. Please tell me you're responsible enough to stay thoroughly hydrated."

"I think I do an okay job of that." He accepted the plate full of food and appreciated the extra spoonful of veggies she gave him. He forked a bite of the chicken into his mouth and paused.

"It's hot," Jamie warned, watching him closely.

Flavors he'd never tasted before bounced about his mouth as he savored the juicy meat. "What in the world did you do to this chicken?"

Her cheeks flushed. "Do you not like it? I can fix you something else."

She quickly started towards her pantry and he reached across the counter to still her movements, his hand gently resting on her arm. "No, no, no... it's amazing." He waited until her eyes met his and he smiled. "I mean, incredibly good."

"Oh." She relaxed into her usual upbeat attitude and lifted her shoulders. "I appreciate good food. And just because I prepare food for other people all day doesn't mean I want to shortchange myself in the evenings. Though I will say, it can quickly add up around the hips, so be careful." She patted a hand against her plump hips and chuckled.

"Ain't nothing wrong with those hips, Red, trust me." Jason complimented, noticing that her fork hesitated a moment before she took a bite of her meal. He ate vigorously and Jamie spooned more onto his plate. "What are you thinking about for tomorrow's breakfast? I can hardly wait to eat it."

Overcoming a sudden wave of shyness, Jamie thought a moment as she chewed. "I could do some quiches. Individual ones. That way there's some good protein again. Or I can do breakfast burritos. Which do you think your crew would like more?"

"Any and all the above. If you make it, they'll eat it." He was beginning to think Jamie was the best cook he'd ever met. "These vegetables, seriously, how do you do this? It's like magic or something. And I consider myself a pretty decent chef when it comes to the basics. But I can't even pinpoint some of these spices."

"Top secret."

"Really?" Disappointed, he glanced up to find her grinning and he chuckled. "Alright, keep your secrets, but don't be surprised if I come beggin' every now and then. Because this plum ruined me of anyone else's cookin'. I can't even fathom wasting my time at the diner now that I've sampled this."

"Flattery will get you nowhere, Mr. Wright," she warned playfully.

"Alright, well then maybe I need to step it up a notch then. Because I'm not meaning to flatter you. I'm stating plain facts." He liked that her cheeks bloomed in color as he continued. When he'd scraped the last of his plate, Jamie placed it in her sink, along with the empty baking dish. He stood. "Not so fast. You cooked. I'll clean up." Invading her space bothered her, he could tell. She awkwardly stepped aside, her hold on the sponge at the sink the last to be given up as he imposed himself in her kitchen. "You sit there." He pointed to the stool he'd just vacated. She reluctantly obeyed. He pumped some fresh soap onto the sponge and began washing the dishes. She watched him carefully. "I like your place."

"Thanks."

"Suits you. Bright and cheerful. I don't think I've ever seen you in a bad mood, even in high school, I don't remember you ever being rude or mean to anyone. And I wasn't always very nice to you. I *do* remember that."

"We were just kids."

"Still, I was kind of a jerk back in those days. Sorry if I was ever awful towards you, Red."

She smirked. "I fill your stomach and you're apologizing for years ago? This evening just took a weird turn."

He shook his head and mustered an embarrassed smile. "I just want you to know I'm grateful for the filling of my stomach, and for being kind to me, even though I haven't always been kind to you. You're a good person, Jamie. I wanted you to know that I appreciate your kindness."

"You're not all bad," Jamie supplied.

He laughed. "Gee, thanks."

"That sounded bad." Jamie rested her tired face in the palm of her hand as she leaned on the counter. "I didn't mean it that way. I meant that you're a nice person too, despite what your reputation or past shenanigans say about you."

"My reputation?" Curiously, he wondered what that might be. He knew parts of it, but he wanted to know the full extent, and what damage control he needed to continue.

She grew uncomfortable at being put on the spot and he waved his hand. "No, tell me."

"I just meant... you know..." She avoided his gaze as she murmured "ladies' man" under her breath.

Yeah, he'd figured that would be one of them. If only she knew... though no one really did. He'd made sure of it. He would much rather people think him a ladies' man or big flirt versus a complete failure at keeping a woman. That something was wrong with him that every woman he'd chosen to love had decided he wasn't good enough, wealthy enough, or just enough, period. No man would own up to that. It put him in check any time he felt even the slightest tendency of getting serious with anyone new. He was cursed at relationships. "There is that one." He nodded in acknowledgement of her comment. "Not everything is as it seems." There. He'd hinted that he wasn't a complete flirt or Casanova. That maybe there was more to him than what people assumed. Not that Jamie would believe it. No one in Piney did. The fact that none of his ex-wives had ever returned to Piney to clear the air had tainted the public's opinion of him with no hope of repair. Thankfully, people didn't let their disapproval of his personal life interfere with hiring him for his professional work. Most of the time, anyway.

"At the reunion you and Leslie Chapin reconnected." Jamie eyed him curiously. "Y'all still keepin' in touch?"

He harumphed. "No. That was just a random meet-up. She seems to have made a good life for herself. Good to see people from the old days doing well. Why do you ask?"

"Was just curious. She seemed... interested that day in the coffee shop."

"Oh." He felt his neck heat up as color climbed to his ears. "Well, I think she may have been. More so than me."

"How do you handle it?" Jamie asked.

"Handle what?"

"Being the target of someone's intentions, pure or not."

"Oh." He shrugged. "Most of the time they aren't really interested. They're just lonely and want extra attention. I'm not really the right person for that. They figure that out pretty quick and then the excuses start. *Well, it's been a long night. Oh goodness, is that the time? Well, it was great catching up.* The list goes on and on. I'm not real big on being someone's fill-in, feel-good, flirt for the day."

"Really?" Jamie's brows lifted.

"No. Would you be?"

"I have no idea. It's never been an issue for me. I'm not exactly the first woman a man looks at when he walks into a room." She admitted it with no vitriol or disdain, just as a statement of fact. She didn't even seem disheartened by it.

But Jason felt for her. As bright a personality, and hair, as Jamie had, she was overshadowed. He wondered if he'd made her feel overlooked in the past. He knew he did. What was he thinking? Of course, he did. And that felt completely crummy.

"Sometimes being noticed isn't all it's cracked up to be, especially if you have a reputation like mine. The boldness of people sometimes surprises me."

"Meaning you're hit on all the time?" Jamie rolled her eyes. "Gee, that must be terrible."

He shook his head. "Not exactly hit on, more like propositioned. And believe it or not, that does feel terrible."

Her face sobered. "Women really go that far?" She reached her hand across the counter and placed it on top of his. "I'm sorry for my tacky response. I guess since I can't relate to even coming close to that sort of problem, I just never thought having people fawning over you would be a negative thing. I guess, in certain circumstances like you're talking about, it would be awful. I've never really looked at it from that angle before." She gasped and then sat up straighter on the stool. "And," She held up a finger. "Completely inappropriate. I've seen a few women drool after Theo over the years, and he was the first to admit it was weird, but he's a good-looking guy, and I just assumed deep-down he kind of liked the extra attention. He didn't. He doesn't. Though Reesa has had a way of building his confidence up a bit more and he's less sensitive about it all. You've always been so confident; I assumed you thrived on the attention. Sorry, Jason."

"No worries, Red. The attention is not all bad, especially when the right kind of woman takes a shine to ya; though I haven't quite found that yet, so I'm not sure what that genuinely feels like."

"You've been married, though. How could you not know?"

"I said *genuinely* feels like. See what I did there?" He air-pointed at the order of his words and she nodded. "Marriage… well, let's just say it's tougher than people make it out to be."

"I wouldn't know." Jamie took a sip of her glass and set it aside. "I've never even come close to walking down the aisle. Serious relationships are hard to keep when you work all the time."

"Tell me about it." Jason pointed to a drawer. "Hand towels?"

"Yep."

He fetched a bright yellow dish towel and began drying the dishes, stacking them neatly on the island top. "Or when you don't want to live in some big, fancy city," he continued.

"Ugh, the worst," Jamie agreed. "My parents still do not understand why I've stayed in Piney. Reminding them that I love it here just isn't enough to cease their worry about me. Apparently, I *dream small*."

"Likewise. Man, Cari, my first wife hated Piney and never could understand why I loved it here so much. Then my second wife, Janessa..." He shook his head. "Well, she hated Piney too. She made sure she waited it out long enough, though, until the opportune time and then high-tailed it out of here. Neither could see the beauty of this place, the people, the way of life. It still baffles me."

"Your first wife was the actress, right?"

"Yes. Still is, I think. Not really sure. I don't keep up with her."
"I'm sorry your marriages didn't work out. I can't imagine how tough that must have been."

He liked that there was no judgment in her tone or on her face. Tiredness was, and though he liked sharing a more personal conversation with Jamie, he could tell she'd hang in there until she plopped her head on the counter and snored her brains out. She was too polite to tell him to leave. But he liked her company, he liked her cozy apartment, and he liked that they'd shared supper together and not once did the conversation hit a dry point. "Well, they weren't meant to be. It's as simple as that." He folded the hand towel. "And on that note, I'm going to get out of that pretty ruby red hair of yours and let you get some rest. I can tell you need it."

Her tired smile and reluctant steps towards the door spoke more for her sleepy state than her words. "I've enjoyed the company. Thanks for hanging around for a bit. It's not every day I get in depth conversations. Most of the time it's "Good morning, what can I get ya?" and move on to the next one. This was refreshing after today."

"I'm glad. Same for me. I yell at sweaty men all day. Supper with a beautiful woman is way better than that."

"Did you just call me beautiful?" Jamie giggled. "Get out of here, you loon. You're as tired as I am if you think this zombie-woman is even remotely beautiful right now." She shooed him out the door and he paused on the other side. "See you bright and early in the morning, Jamie."

"Yes sir. I'll be here. Or there." She pointed beneath their feet at the shop below. "Just follow the lights."

He wriggled his fingers in a spooky gesture at her comment and she grinned. "Night." He tipped his head and carefully descended the stairs.

CHAPTER FIVE

Reesa waved from Charlie's shed as Jamie drove up the driveway towards his house. She parked next to Reesa's little car and then started walking towards her best friend. "It's the big day." Reesa squeezed her around the shoulders as they stepped into the dusty shed and Jamie's eyes adjusted to the dim light. Clare stood beside Charlie, both admiring the 1951 Ford pickup that gleamed in front of them.

"It's red," Jamie pointed out.

"Wow, good eye, Jamie." Reesa smirked as Jamie lightly swatted her.

"Last time I saw the truck it was rusty white. I'm just surprised by the color. Why red?"

"Because I wanted red," Clare stated simply, draping her arm around a sweaty Charlie and leaning her head on his shoulder for a brief second.

"She's spoiled," Reesa muttered, loud enough for all to hear but as if she were telling a secret to Jamie.

"So, is it completely finished?" Jamie asked.

"I believe so." Charlie swiped a handkerchief over his face as Billy Lou's SUV pulled in front of his house. She stepped out in Billy Lou fashion, crisp white capris, gold sandals, and bright blue blouse, her white hair perfectly styled, and her face effortlessly made up. "Good grief that woman is beautiful." Charlie shuffled past all the other women and met Billy Lou halfway. He must have complimented her, because Billy Lou's hand went up to her hair with a small pat and her cheeks lightly flushed.

"Look at them." Clare draped her arms over Reesa and Jamie's shoulders, and they all watched. "They're all grown up."

Laughing, Reesa nudged her daughter aside and pointed at the truck. "There's going to be rules, young lady."

"I know."

"No breaking curfew. No joy riding. No speeding. *Always* wear a seatbelt. Never text and drive."

"I know, Mom. Trust me. Theo's already covered all the bases, though his were more like, 'no boys in the truck, no boys in the back of the truck, no boys under the hood of the truck, no boys breathe on the truck...'" Clare rolled her eyes as Reesa and Jamie laughed.

"Oh, T.J.," Jamie wiped tears from her eyes as she continued to chuckle. "You two have just shaken up his world. Love it."

"Speaking of my gorgeous, tall drink of water," Reesa nodded to the next vehicle to pull up at Charlie's. "There. He. Is." She watched as Theo's long legs swung out of his truck, followed by another pair on the opposite side. "Jason?" Reesa asked. "I wonder what those two have been up to."

Jamie felt a slight stutter in her chest at the sight of a beaming Jason as he shook Charlie's hand and nodded a greeting towards Billy Lou.

While he was standing with his back towards her, Reesa took off in a run and jumped onto Theo's back. He caught her in surprise as she wrapped her arms around his neck and kissed his cheek. Instead of letting her down, he continued to hold her piggy-back style, her chin resting on his shoulder as they spoke with the other adults. "Can't take her anywhere," Clare murmured.

Jamie smiled at her. "You excited about your new ride?"
"I love it." Clare ran a hand down the side of the vintage pickup. "I love that it's a classic. I mean, how cool is that?"

"It is pretty awesome," Jamie agreed.

"And no more begging rides off of everyone."

"We love when you ride with us though," Jamie added. "So, every now and then you have to throw us for a loop and pal around with us."

Clare grinned. "I will." She nodded towards Jason. "I wonder what he and Theo were up to today."

"Oh, I'm sure doing something over at the garage. Jason's got his hands in multiple projects right now, so there's no telling, but that would be my guess."

Jason flashed a smile in their direction, his eyes settling on Jamie, which only made his smile widen.

"Whoa," Clare whispered. "He is so cute."

Jamie turned a surprised look in her direction and the teen shrugged. "What? He is. Annnnd…. He's coming this way. Looks like he's happy to see you." She lightly elbowed Jamie's side before slipping by them with a quick greeting and made her way out of the shed.

"Hey, Red." He ran a hand down the bed of Clare's truck as he approached, whistling in approval at the pretty street rod.

"Hey, yourself. What has you and Theo palling around together?"

"Oh, shop talk." He winked at her as he ran his fingers over his lips like a zipper and then thumbed in Reesa's direction.

"Right." Jamie motioned for them to step out of the shed as well, so she could feel some sunshine and, if she were being honest with herself, have a little more breathing room with Jason.

"I came by your shop to pay you for this morning's feast, but you'd already flipped the sign."

"We can deal with it later," Jamie assured him.

"You have girls' night tonight?"

"No. I just wanted to make sure I was here for the maiden voyage." Jamie nodded towards Clare as she playfully punched Theo in the arm at something he'd said. "And to look at Mr. Charlie's house again. He's offered to rent it to me."

"Really?" Jason turned to face her. "You'd move this far out of town?"

"That's what I'm debating." Jamie looked up at him. "It'd be nice to have the peace and quiet, and some land to enjoy. I've always wanted a garden, but I just don't have the room, as you well know. My little patio can barely hold you, I doubt it can hold rows of crops." She grinned. "I don't know... I've always dreamed of living on a place like this. Maybe now's my chance."

"You realize, if you live here, we'd be neighbors, right?" He pointed to the neighboring pasture. His house was not in view, but across the pasture and through the tree line, she knew it sat on the other side.

"That hadn't crossed my mind. I don't know if I can handle rowdy neighbors." Jamie started to walk closer to the group. "They just cause trouble." She giggled as he nudged her shoulder with his.

"If I knew it was the country life you were seeking, I'd have rented my place to you years ago."

"And where would you live?" Jamie asked.

"I don't know." Jason shrugged. "I've just been wanting a little fresh start somewhere else."

"As in moving out of Piney?" Her eyes widened in shock at his statement, especially after their conversation the other night.

"No, no, I'd stay in Piney. It's just that I grew up in the house I'm living in. I've shared that house with others... I just feel surrounded by memories all the time. I'd like a fresh slate, so to speak. Keep my family's house and property, but maybe rent it out."

"Interesting." Jamie looked at Charlie's house. "You could always rent this one."

"But then where would you live?"

"I'd stay where I'm at. Or I could rent yours, if I wanted to move out this direction so bad."

"A house swap, huh?"

"Well, sort of, I guess. Because Mr. Charlie would move into my loft above my shop. He's wanting to downsize and find a place in town. But the apartments are pretty pricey and he's not sure if he wants to be surrounded by a lot of people, so we'd discussed swapping houses. He'd also be able to keep an eye on the shop for me overnight."

"I see. Well, I wouldn't want to throw a wrench in all those plans. Besides, why would you want my place when you can have a newly renovated place that is much prettier?"

Jamie looked over the country home and sighed. "I do love this place."

"Then there you go." Jason waved his hand for them to continue forwards. "I think I'll like having you as a neighbor, Red."

"It's nothing final, yet," she reminded him. "And you better not bug me all the time."

He laughed. "I'm great at bugging people."

Theo, having caught the last of their conversation, turned and voiced his agreement, Reesa swatted him on the back of his head. "Be nice," she warned, and then kissed where she'd hit him. Theo still held her on his back, and she shifted her head to the opposite shoulder to talk to Jamie. "So, Clare's chosen her first riding buddies, and it's not us."

Jamie gasped and acted wounded.

"I know." Reesa narrowed her eyes at her daughter. "I'm slowly forgiving her."

"Who did she choose?"

"Billy Lou and Charlie."

"Ah, well, you can't fault good taste." Jamie winked at Billy Lou and the older woman laughed and clapped her hands.

"Well, alright, lets load up and get rollin', Clare." Billy Lou walked towards the shed. "I'm ready."

Clare squealed in excitement as she ran towards the shed. She was the first one inside the vehicle and Reesa laughed. "She's feeling the same feelings I did when I sat in your Corvette, Billy Lou. Whispering sweet nothings."

"You're so weird," Theo muttered.

"But you love it," Reesa reminded him and poked him in the cheek.

Theo didn't respond, but the quirk to his lips told her she was exactly right.

"I'm filthy and sweaty. I'm going to change my shirt right quick before we go." Charlie looked to Billy Lou for approval, and she nodded.

"Then we all meet at my house. I've got a celebratory spread just waitin', though you will have to fire up the grill, Theodore. Go." She motioned for Charlie to be quick about changing.

"I'll go hop in with Clare." She opened the door to the classic truck and squealed in excitement as she slid to the middle.

Charlie walked out of the house in a freshly pressed button-down shirt, his face washed, and hair combed. He patted his cheeks. "Well, I'm going to take my girls out for a little spin." He grinned and patted Theo on the shoulder on his way towards the truck. "See y'all at Billy Lou's."

Slowly, the red truck backed out of the shed, the evening sun reflecting off its paint. Jamie snapped several photos as Reesa was too busy crying happy tears. Clare honked the horn, and all passengers waved, as she carefully drove down Charlie's driveway.

"And just like that, she has her wings," Jason commented. "You ready for that, Momma?"

"Absolutely not," Reesa admitted. "But it was bound to happen sooner or later. Who made up the rule that kids have to leave their parents? I mean, why can't we always live together? Why is it so cool to go to college or trade school or beauty school, or whatever? I mean, you put all this work into raising a good human, and then they turn out awesome. And instead of getting to bask in your hard work and hang out with said awesome human forever, you have to send them off to live their own life. I want to keep her."

"Something tells me you won't have a problem keeping Clare nearby. You two have a wonderful relationship," Jamie assured her.

"I know. It just makes me think more and more of my parents over the years." Reesa slid to her feet from Theo's back. "They missed so much. They missed seeing me drive for the first time. They missed seeing me earn my GED. They missed Clare's birth..."

"Different circumstances," Theo reminded her. "And your dad is starting to realize how much he did miss and wants to be a part of your life from now on."

"I know. Still getting used to that one."

"He comes this weekend, right?" Jamie asked, curious to see if Clare and Theo had mentioned Virginia Tate's visit to Piney.

"Yes. And apparently my mom might come." Reesa eyed Jamie.

"Yeah, I wasn't really sure what the protocol was on that. I didn't want to freak you out." Jamie shifted uncomfortably on her feet.

"Don't worry about it. It's probably a good thing you didn't call me and tell me. I would have marched in and not handled that situation well. Since Theo told me, I've been pondering how I'm going to handle it... calmly. Clare seemed rather adamant that she wanted her to come, so what can I say to that? I don't want to deny her the chance to get to know them, but my mama bear instincts are tightly wound right now. I also don't want to see Clare get hurt. So, I'm on guard, but hopeful."

"And I will be there," Theo reminded her.

"You will?" Reesa turned to him in surprise. "I thought you said you were having to be in Hot Springs on Saturday?"

"I'm not going if your parents are both coming to town. I'll be there," he assured her.

"Thanks." Relief washed over Reesa's face as Theo hugged her to his side.

"And if you need me to whip together a dinner or something, just let me know," Jamie offered. "I can drop it off, give an encouraging hug, and then disappear." She fisted her hands on her hips. "Because I want it to go smoothly for all of you. And, honestly, I think it will. Your mother was blown away by Clare the other day. I could tell. And she was... emotional. So, I think having a chance to be around Clare wasn't something she ever even envisioned and will do what she needs to for it to go well." Jason's cell phone rang, and he politely stepped away from the group and answered. His back stiffened, and he paused a moment in his stride, before continuing to separate himself further. Jamie watched him curiously and then turned her attention back to her friends. "I'll meet you guys over at Billy Lou's." Jamie walked towards her car. "Exciting day for Clare today!"

Theo pointed to Jason. "I've got him with me."

"He can come." Reesa smiled and kissed Theo's cheek before she slipped into her car.

"I'll bring him T.J.." Jamie called. "You get over to Billy Lou's. You two are the people Clare will want to see the most when she pulls in."

He nodded his thanks.

"We should make her parallel park," Reesa pondered aloud as she shut the door.

Jamie waited patiently for Jason to turn around so that he would see she was his new ride. He paced back and forth, his steps reluctant, as he listened to the caller. He pulled the phone away from his ear and hung up, tucking it into his back pocket. He stared out over the pasture a moment, taking a few deep breaths before turning to face the crowd. He paused when he saw that it was only Jamie. "Wanna go for a ride, handsome?" she called through the lowered passenger window, playfully whistling until his familiar smile erased the tension on his face.

"Now, how could a man turn that down?" He slid into the passenger side, his long legs eating up the small space, as they headed towards Billy Lou's house.

^

Jason had seen Theo leave the house and ran a hand through his hair in frustration at the woman's voice on the other line. He'd told her, "Listen, I have to go," but her voice continued. "I realize this may have taken you off guard. I just wanted you to know I was coming to Piney and would love to see you." His second wife, Janessa, explained. "Jason?"

"Yeah, thanks for the heads up. Gotta go." He'd hung up and rushed towards Jamie's car, Red's cheerful disposition quickly lifting his spirits. And though she had been forced to be his ride, he wanted to make sure Jamie was okay with it. "Sorry about that." He slid into her passenger seat. "I'm assuming this is okay?" He motioned to his sitting in her car, and she nodded.

"T.J. wanted to be there when Clare pulled in."

"Kind of crazy seeing him in the father role, isn't it?"

"It doesn't surprise me really. T.J.'s always had a big heart."

"Well, yeah. I just meant that less than a year ago he was grumpy, borderline reclusive, and had a chip on his shoulder. Quite the turnaround in a short amount of time."

"The right person, or persons in this case, can do that to a person."

"Or it could go the opposite way too."

"True." Jamie slowly made her way down the bumpy driveway and out onto the small country road. "Just takes wisdom, I guess, to know how someone will affect your life."

"Yeah…" Jason glanced down at his cell phone in regret. "That is definitely something I lacked in my decisions."

Jamie turned to briefly glance in his direction. "Everything okay?" She nodded towards his phone.

"Hm?" He followed her gaze. "Oh. Yeah. Janessa."

"Ex-wife?"

"Yeah. She's apparently coming into town."

"Does she come often?" Jamie asked.

"No. I haven't seen her since our divorce two years ago."

"Oh." Jamie grew quiet and navigated her way towards Billy Lou's house.

"Yeah, I don't know what she could possibly want here in Piney. Her family is long gone. The only thing here is—"

"Is what?"

"Me." Jason cleared his throat and focused his attention on the tree line outside his window.

"You don't seem excited." Jamie absentmindedly reached into her cup holder, withdrew a peppermint, and popped it into her mouth.

"I'm not. That woman took me for everything I had."

She turned wide eyes in his direction. "What?"

"I literally just paid off the last of her debts last week. The last thing I want is to see her after what she's put me through."

"It's taken you two years to pay off her debt? What did she buy? A yacht?"

"She bought everything and anything."

"And why is she not having to pay it off?"

"Oh, I'm sure she is. No telling how much debt she has in her own name, this was just what she took out in mine."

"Jason…" Jamie reached over and squeezed his hand. "I had no idea. That's a big burden for sure. I'm sorry you were left with that."

"Small price to pay in the end. I'm just glad I found out when I did. I was completely enraptured to the point of blindness. It's taken me two years of busting my rear to pay off her debts, replenish my accounts that she drained, and Theo's new project will help set me ahead of where I was at before I married her. I've climbed my way out of it all, it's just taken me a while. Just penance, I guess, for being so blind and stupid."

"You were in love with her. That wasn't stupid. What was stupid, was her screwing it up."

He smirked and caught her understanding gaze. "Thanks for that."

"What can I say? You're growing on me."

"Just taken twenty years though, right?"

She laughed, her light giggle instantly brightening his mood. "Oh, I always liked you," Jamie added. "You were just a pain in the butt sometimes."

"Ugh. I was, wasn't I? I'm sorry if I ever caused you grief, Red. You're one of the best people I know, and over the years, my stomach gets all twisted when I think of any of the times I was awful to you in high school."

Baffled, Jamie scoffed. "What? Jason, that was a long time ago. I hope you know I don't hold a grudge."

"I know you don't, because you're too kind to. I'm just apologizing and letting you know I appreciate your friendship despite my awfulness."

"We all grow up at some point." Jamie pulled in behind Reesa's car and parked, turning to Jason and placing a hand on his arm before he could exit the vehicle. "Look, you're a wonderful man, Jason. You work hard, you're friendly, you love this town and help make it a better place. Don't let Janessa come and rob you of that. She can't take that from you unless you let her."

Jason reached out and lightly brushed a knuckle down her smooth cheek and he watched as a nice rush of pink flooded them in his wake. "Thanks, Red. Can I just shrink you down and carry you in my shirt pocket? That way when I'm having a bad day I can just whip you out and have you encourage me."

Jamie grinned. "I'm always available. You know where to find me, because I doubt I'd ever fit in a shirt pocket." She giggled as she slid out of her car and waited for him to do the same.

He draped his arm over her shoulders as they walked towards Billy Lou's porch to the awaiting Reesa and Theo. Reesa handed Jamie a metal cow bell. "We're going to go crazy when she pulls in," Reesa explained.

"Oooooh I love ringing cowbells." Jamie tested it out and both Jason and Theo cringed at the sound.

"Oh look, here they come!" Reesa pointed and began frantically waving the cowbell as she ran into the middle of the yard and cheered as her daughter successfully pulled into the driveway and parked. Clare's cheeks flamed pink, but she accepted the excited hug from her mother. "How was it?"

"Awesome." Clare hugged Theo as he walked up, and then Jamie. She eyed Jason curiously before going ahead and hugging him as well.

"Well, she followed every rule and is quite graceful behind the wheel," Billy Lou complimented. "Despite this one tempting her to test her speed," she scolded Charlie with a firm gaze, and he grinned.

"Had to see how she'd react to a handsome man trying to bait her. She withstood the temptation to show off."

Clare grinned happily as Billy Lou waved them towards her house.

"Come on now, it's time to celebrate!"

Jason's cell phone rang again, and he reached into his pocket with an apologetic expression at interrupting the mood. No one paid him any mind except Jamie. He glanced at the screen, silenced the call, and sent it straight to voicemail.

"Again?" Jamie asked.

He flushed at her seeing him ignore Janessa's call. "Um, yeah."

"Good thing you're busy the next few days. Maybe you won't even have to see her."

"I can only hope," he sighed. "Gosh, that makes me sound like a jerk."

"No, it doesn't. It sounds like you know how to set up healthy boundaries. And sometimes, as much as we hate to, we have to do that. Now, come on. I don't know about you, but I relish the chance to eat so of Billy Lou's cookin'."

"I don't know... she'd have to be mighty good to beat yours." He liked that his compliment caused her cheeks to flush, and he grinned as they entered the large, open kitchen.

"Pull up a stool, Jason, don't be shy now." Billy Lou pointed to a seat next to Theo and he obliged with a nod of his head as Reesa slid him a glass of iced tea. He nodded his thanks as he watched Jamie don an apron and hop into the fray with Billy Lou. He liked that she listened to Billy Lou's wishes, directions, and even corrections in a gracious manner. Jamie knew her way around a kitchen, and she was an excellent chef in her own right, but her humility and recognition of Billy Lou's authority in her own kitchen spoke volumes for her character. Her capable hands worked diligently as she cut thick slices of bread and slathered them in butter. She placed them on a baking sheet and walked them over to the double oven and slid them into the top oven and set the timer. She then walked back and accepted the cutting board and tomatoes from Billy Lou and began dicing tomatoes for the salad.

"If you stare any harder, she's going to notice." Reesa's whisper caught him off guard as did her close presence as she leaned on the island next to him with an amused smirk on her face.

Jason quickly diverted his gaze to his cup and took a long sip.

"Atta boy. Cool off," Reesa teased, patting him on the back on her way towards Theo. She kissed Theo's cheek in passing as she wound her way over to Clare and Charlie, where they sat building a puzzle at the small dinette table.

"I should go." Jason stood and everyone paused to look in his direction.

"Why on earth would you leave now? We're about to eat?" Billy Lou motioned for him to sit back down.

"I appreciate that, Ms. Billy Lou, but I—"

"Posh!" Billy Lou waved away his excuse. "Did something life or death come up?"

"No ma'am. I just—"

"Then you're stayin'." She pointed to his stool. "Don't deprive me of the opportunity of cookin' for you. Nothing irritates me faster than someone who leaves on an empty stomach."

"Best get comfortable," Theo mumbled.

"Clare," Billy Lou called out. "You get first plate, sweetie. Come on now, Charlie. Leave that puzzle for later. Let's eat while it's hot. Jamie, darlin', the bread done?"

Jamie pulled the pan out of the oven. "Yes ma'am." She brought it over to the island and slid the slices into an awaiting basket.

"Good. Let's say grace, Theo," Billy Lou directed. "With an extra prayer of protection over Clare and that pickup."

"Yes ma'am." Theo, along with everyone else in the room, bowed their heads.

Jason eyed Jamie across the island, and as if sensing someone looking at her, she glanced up, her blue eyes surprised to find his. She offered an encouraging smile before closing her eyes once more until Theo said, "Amen."

Clare took great pleasure in choosing the first of the chicken quarters and all the sides to go with it, though she did offer Reesa a deviled egg on her way by to tide her mother over until it was her turn.

Jason followed Theo and watched as Jamie carried her plate to the large dining table and found a seat. He walked over and placed his plate next to hers. She looked up in surprise. "Mind if I sit by you, Red?"

"Not at all." She watched as he set his tea down and realized she didn't have one of her own.

"Don't. I'll get you one. Tea?"

"Yes, please. Thanks." She smiled up at him as she began eating her food. Reesa sat across from her and nodded towards Jason's plate. And though he couldn't hear what she was saying, he could tell Jamie was not open for the discussion by her shushing her friend's conversation when he walked up. He handed Jamie her drink.

"So, Jason, how are all your projects going?" Reesa asked.

"Pretty good. They're keeping me busy, and that's always good."

"You and Theo seem to be getting along," Reesa baited. "His project not that complicated?"

Jason bit back a smile. "I'm not going to tell you what he's working on."

"Argh." She tossed a piece of bread at him. "Fine. Keep your secrets. Secrets are bad for business, you know."

He laughed and turned to call over his shoulder. "Theo, Reesa won't leave me alone about your shop."

"You rat," Reesa hissed playfully.

"He's not telling you either," Theo assured her.

"Ugh, why not? Why do you have to be so secretive about it if it's 'not that big a deal'?"

"Because it's fun." Theo smirked as Reesa rolled her eyes. "And it drives you crazy."

"You know, Theo," Reesa began, "It's not smart to purposely annoy your significant other. Hasn't anyone ever taught you that?"

"I'm afraid I missed that lesson. That's why I'm so good at it."

Reesa bit back a laugh as she grinned. "Fine. I'll stop pestering Jason about it, then." She leaned conspiratorially across the table. "Though, if you want an extra muffin tomorrow morning from Jamie's, I could possibly hook you up." She winked.

"Now she's bribing me, Theo," Jason added.

Theo shot Reesa a look and she beamed. "You're going to have to tell me sooner or later."

"Just do it, Theo," Clare interrupted. "Or else she's only going to get worse, and I don't want her to ruin her shot."

Theo's lips twitched at Clare's response, and he studied her for a moment until she gave a firm nod for him to go ahead.

He sighed, then stood to his feet and motioned for Reesa to come towards him. "If I tell you, will you please let everyone eat in peace?"

"I will do my best." She grinned and tossed a smile over her shoulder to Jamie and Jason. When she turned around, she gasped. "W-what are you doing?" She looked at a kneeling Theo in wonder as he reached into his back pocket and withdrew a small box. He flicked the lid open to reveal an antique diamond ring. Billy Lou stood to the side, her hands over her heart as she watched.

"Reesa—" Theo's deep voice caught a moment, and he cleared his throat as he looked up at her. Tears streamed down her cheeks as she looked to her daughter. Clare's eyes began to water as well as Billy Lou hugged her around the shoulders. "I've thought about what I was going to say when I finally did this," Theo continued. "And no matter what I come up with in my head, none of it seems enough." He swiped a nervous hand over his mouth as he looked up at Reesa and grabbed her hand in his. "You've changed my life. The both of you have." He turned and flashed a look at Clare before returning his attention to Reesa. "If it weren't for you two, I'd still be shut off from the world and just living in my own world. Well, really, I wasn't even living. I was just existing, going through the day to day. You've made me reevaluate what's important. You've made me want things I never even thought possible. And you've made me a better man. My deepest wish is that you'll let me take care of you and love you for the rest of my days. Will you marry me?"

"Yes!" Reesa waited patiently for him to slip the ring on her finger and then embraced him, kissing him passionately, until Charlie cleared his throat. Breathless, Theo beamed as Reesa grabbed Clare and pulled her into a hug. Theo reached into his other back pocket and withdrew a slender box and held it out to Clare.

Her eyes widened at the gift, and she opened it and grinned. She withdrew a silver chain with a small charm shaped like a wrench. She hugged Theo tightly around the middle.

Jamie watched in silence, tears streaming down her own face at watching her friends come together. Jason reached over and squeezed her hand and she jolted at his touch before returning it.

"We're going to have some big news for Grandma and Grandpa this weekend," Clare laughed as she swiped tears from her eyes.

Reesa smiled and then withdrew from Theo just enough to look up at him and then to Jason. "Wait... this still doesn't answer my question on what you two are up to at the garage?"

"Oh, right...." Theo rubbed a hand over his jaw and grinned. "It's a carwash."

"I *knew* it!" Reesa swatted him on the chest. "You big sneak!"

"To be fair, I was never sneaky. You can clearly see what's happening there."

"But why the big secret?" Reesa asked.

"My hope was to finish it and then ask you to marry me when I revealed it to you," Theo explained. "But you're so pushy, I had to do it now and ruin the grand gesture."

She laughed as he kissed her soundly on the mouth to show he wasn't in the least bit annoyed.

"So much to celebrate!" Billy Lou clapped her hands together and snuggled into Charlie's side as he walked up next to her. "Good thing I made cake!"

CHAPTER SIX

Jamie listened as Reesa's crochet hook made soft sliding sounds through her yarn, and the gentle tugging sound the skein made each time Reesa pulled for slack. It was the first time she'd let Reesa work inside her studio as she painted. But considering Jamie was painting a picture of Clare, she'd wanted to invite Reesa in for her approval. "No big date set yet?"

"He just proposed yesterday," Reesa laughed. "I think if I were to already bombard Theo with a date, he might shy away."

"Possibly true." Jamie grinned as she swished her brush across the canvas and rounded downward to form the front curve of Clare's pickup. "Still can't believe how romantic T.J. was, just dropping down on his knee like that."

"I know, right?" Reesa sighed happily and set her crochet down as she watched Jamie in silence for a few moments. "I'm still in awe that I'm actually engaged."

"You two deserve all the happiness I know you'll have."

"Thanks." Reesa went back to her work. "You're going to be in our wedding, right?"

"Duh." Jamie giggled as she turned to look at Reesa and then gasped. Jason stood in the doorway watching them work. "Jason! What are you doing here?" She quickly set her paintbrush aside and hopped to her feet, blocking the view of her painting.

"What in the world?" He stepped across the threshold into the small studio space and spun in circles looking at all of Jamie's paintings and supplies in wonder. "This room has been here this whole time?" He pointed at the floor beneath his feet as he studied a landscape painting on the wall and then eyed the rough shaping of Clare and her new truck on the canvas on her easel. "Jamie, this is... I didn't know you could do this. I mean, I saw Charlie's painting, but I didn't know you were capable of all this." He motioned his hand to the entire room.

"I, uh, I paint," Jamie announced.

"No kidding." He beamed at her and then shook his head in disbelief. "You continue to surprise me, Red."

"How did you get into the shop?" Jamie asked.

"The door was unlocked." He motioned over his shoulder. "I just assumed you left it open for me to come pay you for this morning's breakfast."

"No..." Jamie looked disappointed.

Jason held a hand to his heart. "Did I do something wrong?"

She quickly masked her frustration and shook her head. "No, no, you are completely fine. I just... I don't really let anyone see this room."

"Reesa is here."

"First time," Reesa stated as she looked up from her rows and watched them.

"Oh. Well, I'm sorry if I overstepped." Jason's handsome face fell slightly, and Jamie didn't like that she'd made him feel unwanted.

"You didn't. I'm just weird about it, that's all." She motioned for him to step back into the shop area. "How'd the guys like those mini quiches? I added mushrooms this time." She squealed at the thrill of having fresh mushrooms and he laughed.

"They loved them, of course. And they're feeling quite spoiled now."

"Good."

Jason withdrew his company checkbook and wrote her a check for the amount on his invoice, plus extra, and handed it to her.

"Is this a tip?" She fluffed her hair and he grinned.

"Yes, because you truly do go the extra mile. Now, want me to bring in the decanters?"

"Sure. I can help you. Reesa! I'll be right back."

"Take your time." Reesa's muffled response sounded distracted, and Jamie followed him out the door.

"She's working on a new pattern. Lots of counting."

Jason opened his passenger door, and fished out two decanters, and placed them in Jamie's arms as he reached inside for the remaining two. "Jason?" A female voice drifted towards them, and his head snapped up, regret briefly flashing across his face, before he plastered a polite smile on his face. "Janessa." Jamie gaped a moment before collecting herself, and she started to walk back to her shop. "Please, wait," he whispered to her as Janessa walked towards them. The woman was smartly dressed in black leggings and an oversized cream sweater, dainty sandals, and hooped earrings. Her makeup was impeccable, and Jamie doubted the woman had ever eaten a carbohydrate. She looked the part of supermodel, and Jamie suddenly felt frumpy in comparison.

"I've tried to reach you." Janessa's eyes soaked him in and then they travelled over to Jamie. "Do you mind? I'd like to speak to Jason alone for a minute."

Jamie looked to Jason, torn between being polite and also following his wishes. His smile was pained, but he nodded to her that she was free to leave him on his own. "I'll be just a minute, Red."

Jamie nodded and hurried into her shop, placing the decanters on the back counter as Reesa stepped out of the studio. "Ex-wife is on the premises."

"What?" Reesa snuck a glance out the front window as she pretended to help Jamie dismantle the decanters. "Which one?"

"The second, I believe," Jamie added.

"Wow! I forget he's been married so many times."

"Two is not that many."

"Really?" Reesa eyed her curiously. "And what would you consider a lot?"

"I just meant... well, maybe he just has bad luck."

"The more I get to know him, I don't understand why he hasn't stayed married. He seems like a great guy." Reesa watched as Jamie rinsed out a decanter and flipped it to dry in the sink.

"He is a great guy," Jamie defended. "And he's worked very hard to recover from the damage she caused him. I hope he keeps a level head."

"What do you mean damage?" Reesa asked.

"Not my business to share," Jamie added, already regretting the tidbit she slipped.

"Sounds like you two have gotten to be pretty good friends lately," Reesa prodded. "I noticed you guys were a little chummy at Billy Lou's yesterday."

"We've known each other a long time." Jamie walked to the storage closet and came back with coffee supplies to prep for the next morning when she would refill the decanters for Jason.

"Do you have a little spark for Mr. Wright?" Reesa asked.

"What?" Jamie glanced up in surprise. "Why would you say that?"

"Because your face turned the color of Clare's pickup when I just said that," Reesa observed. "Come on, Jamie, you can tell me."

"It's nothing. I've been cooking for his crew for the week. We've seen a lot more of each other, that's all. I guess that would make it seem like we've gotten to know one another better or feel more comfortable around one another."

"You sure that's it?" Reesa asked.

"Positive." Jamie nodded with forced enthusiasm.

"Okay, good. Not that I don't like Jason or anything," Reesa continued. "He's just... well, his reputation and all. I wouldn't want to see you get your heartbroken by a well-known player."

Jamie's insides twisted and she felt an immediate defense for Jason rise in her chest, but she tamped it down and flashed a quick smile to her friend. "Don't worry about me. Right now, I'm just enjoying the extra income he's bringing me."

Her answer sufficient, Reesa walked back into the studio to continue her work and left Jamie dilly-dallying behind her counter. She cast a glance every now and then to make sure Jason and Janessa still stood out in front of the shop. She wasn't sure if she should intervene in some way or let him be. His quiet pleading for her to stay outside had squeezed her heart, his nerves betraying him before he'd turned and faced Janessa. She'd never seen Jason so vulnerable, but she also did not want to get mixed up in whatever issues or unfinished business he had with his ex-wife. Yet seeing them outside the window, and how they looked standing near one another, Jamie's heart saddened. They fit. They looked great together. And though she could stand in her shop all night and say he was an old friend or a business perk for this quarter's numbers, she had begun to feel a little drawn towards Jason. She'd liked getting to know him better and that they shared their evenings and mornings together, however briefly. She'd enjoyed it and looked forward to it, but she had to remain realistic. Jason Wright had never once looked her way for more than friendship, and she doubted that would ever change. And with his ex-wife back in town, she knew their short-lived 'chummier' friendship would fade away, and with it any hope that he might have asked Jamie out.

"It's awfully late for you to be getting coffee, isn't it?" Janessa asked, her eyes observing the exterior of Jamie's shop and then the decanters in his truck floorboard.

"My business." Jason crossed his arms and studied her for a moment.

"You look good." Janessa smiled. "The last couple of years seem to have treated you well."
"I'd like to think so."

"And Jamie as well. Her shop looks cute. That was the same Jamie you went to high school with, right?"

"It is."

"I vaguely remember her selling coffee out of a food truck."

"She used to."

"Huh... good for her." Janessa flashed a quick smile.

"What are you up to, Janessa?" Jason asked. "I know it's not to have small talk., so why are you in town?" He leaned against the hood of his truck and crossed his arms over his chest. Janessa nervously tucked her hair behind her ear and fidgeted with her hands. He used to love that habit of hers, but now when he watched her, he felt nothing but annoyance at her interfering with his evening. He flashed a quick glance towards the coffee shop and saw Jamie working away behind her counter, laughing at something Reesa must have shouted from the adjoining room. His lips quirked at seeing Jamie bust a silly dance move before going about her business.

"I need your help." Janessa's voice cut through his thoughts, and he looked back at her.

"Wrong person to ask." Jason thumbed over his shoulder. "I should get back."

"Jason, come on." Janessa's smile wavered as she reached towards him.

He avoided her touch and held up his hands. "What? Come on, what? After all you left me with? Goodness, just leaving me was bad enough, but to leave me in ruins as well, and then you want to come and ask me for help? Why on Earth would you even think I would want to help you, Janessa?"

"I just... well... it's Jarin."

Jason's face held no recognition.

"*Our son*," she stressed. "We have a son."

The breath left Jason's lungs and he gaped. "What?"

Her eyes soaked in his stunned reaction.

"We have a kid?" Jason asked. "W-w-why did you not tell me? How old is he? Where is he?"

She motioned over her shoulder towards her sleek black car. "He's asleep in the backseat."

"We have a son together," he stated again for clarification. His knees felt weak, and he eased onto the curb and sat, his stomach twisting at the thought of being a father to a child he had no idea existed until that moment. "Why did you not tell me until now?"

Janessa sighed and leaned her back against his truck as she looked down at him. "We were done. You made it clear you didn't want anything to do with me after I left, and well, when I found out I was pregnant, life was good, and I felt like I could do it on my own."

"I had a right to know." Jason shook his head at her flippant answer and stared at the back window of her car imagining how his entire world would change once he opened the door and gazed upon his child. Suspicion slipped into his thoughts. "How do I know he's mine?"

Janessa's back stiffened. "Really? Why would I lie about this?"

He looked at her with narrowed eyes and she sputtered.

"Well, I wouldn't about this. Trust me. I did not want to come back to Piney, of all places. I hate this place. Besides, I don't care if you want a paternity test to prove it. Go for it. I'm telling you, once you see him, you will know he is your son." She walked over to her car and opened the back passenger door; a small figure buckled into the chair stirred at the sudden gust of wind that fluttered through the car. She began unsnapping and unclipping buckles and scooped the small boy into her arms. He woke with a grumble, burying his neck in her hair to try and find a comfortable position to fall back to sleep.

Jason stood to his feet as she walked the child over to him and gently shook his elbow to wake him up. "Jarin," she whispered. "Look here. I have someone I want you to meet."

The little boy blinked at her and then slowly turned his face towards him, and Jason's heart dropped. The little boy was his miniature. There was no denying that he was his son. He looked exactly like Jason did as a child and his blue eyes searched Jason's face with uncertainty.

"We just need a place to stay for a bit," Janessa continued. "I got a little behind on rent and my landlord locked us out of my apartment."

"I need a minute." Jason scooped up the remaining coffee decanters and hurried into the coffee shop. The bell and the slap of the door closing behind him with force had Jamie's brow scrunching together as she glanced up. "Sorry," he grumbled, walking towards her. He set the decanters on the counter and gripped the edge with his hands before hanging his head and inhaling two long deep breaths. He reached for his checkbook. "How much was it again?" he asked.

"You already paid me, Jason." Jamie reached across the counter and patted one of his hands. "You okay?"

He ran a hand through his hair and forced a mangled smile and she shook her head and stifled a laugh. "If you think that is going to convince me, you are sadly mistaken."

"Jamie... I have to go. I just... needed a breather and... a friend for a minute."

Concern had her setting her dish towel aside. "Janessa still out there?" she asked. "Do I need to go out there and tell her to leave? Because I will. This is my place of business and technically she is parked in one of my designated spots." Her hackles rose and he loved that she'd be willing to take on Janessa, or anyone, on his behalf.

"No, but thank you. I—" he rubbed a nervous hand over his mouth before speaking the words aloud. "I have a son."

Jamie's face blanched in surprise before she reached across the counter and gripped both his hands. "Congratulations." His misery at the newfound information changed her usual friendly demeanor to sympathy. "That's a lot to take in..."

"It is." Jason looked up at her. "I... I don't know what to do. I mean, obviously I'll do *something*, I just don't know what to do."

"Is he out there?" Jamie asked.

Jason nodded.

"Then you meet him. You smile at him. You make him feel safe. You're a stranger to him too. I imagine he is a bit nervous or scared as well."

"I didn't even think of that. And I have no idea what she's told him or how much he understands. He's little. Probably two-ish." He rambled and

Jamie patted his hands again, bringing his attention back to her kind gaze.

"Go out there, Jason. This is the most pivotal moment for the both of you. It's important that you be there for it."

"You're right. I know you're right. But... I don't know how to do this." He straightened and his usual confidence fled as he thought about what it meant to be a father. He had no clue. He'd never even read a parenting book in his life.

Reesa quietly walked into the room and Jason felt the heat rise in his cheeks at the extra audience. She held up her hand as if she came in peace. "I'm sorry to overhear."

He bit back a retort because his emotions were too raw, and he knew he needed to go back outside before Janessa lost patience and left.

"We've got your back in this," Jamie said. "If they stay in Piney and you need help, a friend, or even a meal, we've got you."

Reesa nodded.

Jason stared at the two women in front of him and wondered how he'd gotten so lucky to now call them friends. Moved by their offer of support, he nodded his thanks.

"The best thing in my life is Clare," Reesa stated. "Even when it was hard, she made it easy. Even when I had no idea what I was doing, she made all the struggle, uncertainty, and fear worth it. Still does."

Jason felt a sob rise in the back of his throat, and he choked it back on a cough and pinched the bridge of his nose until he'd collected himself. He nodded his head and took a deep breath. "I'm going back out there. Thank y'all for..." He trailed off, not even knowing what to say.

"You're welcome," Jamie finished. "Now go. Meet your son." She beamed at him, and he slowly made his way back out the door.

Janessa turned as she swayed on her feet, rocking their son who laid his head on her shoulder and stared at Jason with wide eyes as his thumb slowly made his way to his mouth.

"Alright, I'll help you out," Jason announced. "But just for a little while. You can stay in the guest room at the farm."

Relief washed over Janessa's face, and she nodded. "Thank you."

"But tomorrow morning, you're going to explain to me why you kept this a secret and you're going to tell me how you plan to get back on your feet."

"I will." She walked the boy back to her car and buckled him in his seat, his eyes never leaving Jason.

Jason offered a shaky smile at him and lifted a hand. "Just follow me." He climbed into his truck and headed home with his heart heavy and his mind whirling.

CHAPTER SEVEN

"*Wow.*" *Jamie turned a* shocked expression to Reesa as they watched Jason and Janessa leave the parking lot.

"Quite a shock for him." Reesa sighed and motioned to the decanters he'd brought in. "Want me to help wash?"

"That's okay." Jamie walked them over to her sink. "You go on home. I'm sure Clare and T.J. are wondering where you're at by now."

"Negative, Ghost Rider," Reesa replied, her typical movie-quoting response eliciting a chuckle from Jamie. "Theo knows I'm working on finishing a pattern. Clare knows I will obsess over it until it's completed and is, I'm sure, sharing her wisdom to

Theo as he paces, annoyed, across my living room waiting for me to get home."

"And yet, here you are." Jamie glanced over her shoulder at her friend. "Everything okay?"

"Yep." Reesa nodded. "I'm engaged to a super-hot, moody, broody, mechanic who thinks the world of me. I can't complain. I'm just overwhelmed right now. I feel like I can't truly celebrate my engagement when I have a pattern deadline looming. And with my mom coming up this weekend, let's just say I'm a bit on edge."

"Yeah, so what are you guys going to do?"

"Figured I'd whip together a barbecue. Well, let's be honest, I will have Theo do that. Have a nice meal, and then maybe invite my best friend over to hang out in the evening." Reesa pleaded with her hands clasped together and Jamie smiled.

"I'd love to come by. Just text me when you're ready for me."

"Sounds good. I'll get out of your hair. Maybe if Theo sees I'm still in one piece after disappearing for hours, he'll calm down enough to go home. I'll stay up too late working on this pattern, come here in the morning and beg you for caffeine. Then, I'll stop by his garage, delivering *him* some caffeine, all while fitting in my morning eyeful of dreamy mechanic." Reesa beamed. "My morning is filling up fast."

Jamie giggled. "Does Theo realize your morning drop-ins are just to check him out?"

"No. If he did, he'd be all awkward about it." Reesa's smile turned tender. "My shy mechanic. He's so cute."

Laughing, Jamie walked her to the door. "Well, I will see you in the morning, then. Be careful heading home."

"Yep. See ya." Reesa shouldered her crochet tote and walked to her car. She offered one last wave before backing out onto the dark street.

Jamie locked her door and turned off the lights to the main room. She then walked to her studio and diligently put away her paints, washed her brushes, and cleaned her space. She studied her portrait of Clare and liked how it was coming along. Already, she could see Clare's body language coming through the figure and she liked that she was able to capture that slight teenage slouch with Clare's confident shoulders. She turned off the light, exited the back room, and headed up her creaky stairs. She'd take a long bubble bath to calm down, her mind too worked up after the night's events. Jason had a kid. The surprise of that had her heart twisting. "Don't be ridiculous, Jamie," she scolded herself. "You can't be upset about it. It's a blessing in disguise for him. You can't be selfish." She unlocked her door and stepped inside her cozy home, sighing in relief at the smell of her supper cooking in the slow cooker. She'd forgotten she'd done that. "Bath first, then eat," she announced to her room. She kicked off her shoes and placed them on the bench by the door before walking towards her bathroom. "I'm not upset," she repeated to herself. "I'm not upset." Her words quieted to a whisper as she felt disappointment gather behind her eyes and begin to sting. She would not cry. Had she enjoyed getting to know Jason better? Yes. Had she thought he'd started to see her as a good friend, possibly, maybe even a little more than that? Oddly, yes. But now? Now that Janessa was back, and with his son, there was no chance Jamie would get to know him further. And despite knowing she never stood a chance, she was still upset. Upset with herself for believing she did. And upset that she'd started to hope and enjoy the extra time and attention from him. She sighed as the hot water rose above her toes and the smell of lavender and lemongrass soothed her raw emotions. She'd wake up early, complete his order for his crew put on a smile like she always did, and treat him like any other customer.

She wasn't sure how long she'd laid in the water. Long enough that she awoke with a jolt; the heat had all disappeared and she shivered in the cold bath. She stood and toweled off, donning her favorite pj pants and top before shuffling to the kitchen and making herself a quick bowl of soup. She turned off the cooker and ate in the quiet. She'd normally watch an episode or two of her favorite show, but tonight she just felt blah. "Blah blah blah," she stated aloud and then shimmied her shoulders to try and shake off the mood. She couldn't. She didn't like that, but she knew it would take a while for her to wash away her disappointed hopes. She washed her bowl, placing it on the dish cart to dry and walked over to her bookshelf. Perhaps a little Jane Austen would set her mood right again. It was hard not to feel hope when reading Pride and Prejudice. Mr. Darcy's reluctant fall over Elizabeth made even the hardest of hearts giddy. She plucked it off the shelf and walked to her room. Settling into her fluffy duvet, she shrieked when a pounding on her front door had her fumbling her book and scurrying out of bed. She cautiously walked over to the door, her eyes glancing at the clock on the wall. It was well after midnight, and she couldn't fathom why anyone would be knocking on her door. When she glanced out of the peephole, she only saw a shadow.

"Jamie, it's me. Jason." Jason's voice carried through the thick door and her fingers made quick work at the locks. She opened to a wide-eyed, panicked Jason Wright.

"Jason, what are you doing here?"

He barreled past her, his hands in his hair, as he paced back and forth. "Gone."

"What?"

"She's gone." He pointed out the door and Jamie glanced outside and only saw the headlights of his truck parked haphazardly behind her shop next to her car, the engine still running and his door ajar as he'd sprinted up her steps.

"Okay, slow down. Who is gone? Janessa?"

"Yes." He walked back out the door and pointed to his truck. "She left."

"Alright..." Jamie placed a calming hand on his arm, and he turned wild eyes in her direction that had her quickly retreating.

"I-I-I don't know what to do. I'm... I'm not even sure how to do this. I mean, I'm not a dad. I don't know what to do. How do I do this?" His frantic words jumbled over one another as he stepped down towards his truck and then back up to Jamie. He gripped her hands. "I need your help, Jamie."

She stared into his terrified blue eyes and felt herself nod. Relief washed over him instantly and he pulled her into a tight hug. "Thank you. Thank you. Thank you." His words were mumbled into her hair. He released her and hurried down the steps to his truck and opened his back door. He reached inside and then a rumpled toddler was in his arms as he made his way up the stairs. Jamie's eyes widened in surprise.

"Wait. She left him with you?"

Jason nodded, his nervous hands shifting the sleeping boy from one side to the other.

"Come inside." Jamie led the way towards her bedroom and watched as Jason laid the small boy on her bed and his nervous hands attempted to tuck him in. Jamie helped, the little boy adjusting quickly to his new surroundings. His eyes flickered open a moment and studied Jamie before they drifted closed again and he slept.

Jason and Jamie walked into her living room, and she quietly closed her bedroom door. Jason paced back and forth, his long legs eating up the tiny space. "You need to calm down," she stated softly.

His eyes flickered in her direction, and he shook his head as he gripped the tips of his hair as if attempting to pull any kind of response from his brain.

"Jason," she said again, and walked towards him. She reached up, gently grabbed his hands, and led him to her couch. "Sit."

He obeyed, though his grip on her hands tightened.

"Tell me what happened."

He inhaled a deep, calming breath, his eyes studying hers. "Okay."

"Okay," she encouraged.

"I took them back to my place because Janessa said they didn't have any money to get a hotel or anything. So, I let them stay in my guest room."

"Alright."

"Nothing happened. I mean, between us... Janessa and me. I just simply let her have a room to sleep in and we were going to discuss things more in the morning."

"Sounds wise."

"I woke up about an hour ago because the kid... wow, that sounds awful. My son, his name is Jarin..." he babbled. "Jarin was crying. I mean, *really* crying and screaming. I didn't get up right away because I thought maybe he just woke up in a new place and was scared and figured Janessa would handle it. But he just kept crying. And screaming. I finally got up and went in there and he was alone. Janessa was gone."

"Did she—"

"Oh yeah." He pulled a piece of paper out of his back pocket. "Left this note on the nightstand." He handed it to her and motioned for her to read it. Jamie slowly unfolded the note, and her eyes ate up the words of the desperate woman.

Jason,

I've tried, but I'm just not cut out for this. He is your son. I know you can tell by looking at him. I'm sorry things have come to this, but I cannot do this anymore. I'm not meant to be a mother. I never wanted to be. He's yours. I know you will give him a better life than I can. You were always honorable, and I know Jarin is in good hands with you. Please don't try to find me.

Janessa

"I have no idea what to do, Red." Jason leaned back against the cushions of the couch and covered his face with his hands before dragging them through his hair. "Part of me is questioning whether or not this is even real, but I know it is. And she's right... that boy is mine. There's no denying it. He looks just like me. I mean, I guess I could have a paternity test done to be sure, but he truly does look just like I did at that age, and he favors what I look like now."

"I did notice he had blue eyes like you."

Jason's lips thinned into a straight line instead of a smile as she saw him try to maintain his composure.

"She left a folder in his suitcase, birth certificate inside. She never intended to stay. She came by only to drop him off and leave him. Poor kid. I don't know what I'm going to tell him tomorrow."

"You'll think of something." Jamie patted his knee and he sighed, leaning towards her and placing his forehead against the back of her hand. "I'm sorry to just turn up like this. You were the first person I could think of that would... I don't know... be here... for me." He lifted his head and sat back. "I needed some Jamie Bishop light." She smiled as he searched her face. "I'm at a loss, Red. I have no clue how to be a dad. I have no clue what the first step is tomorrow. I have no clue if I go to the authorities or if I just do as she asks and let her go. I mean, what *is* the right move?"

"Honestly? I have no idea." Her answer had his eyes glassing over as a new wave of panic seemed to surface. She reached a calming hand over to his and gripped his fingers. "But hey, we'll figure it out together. I have the perfect person to call in the morning. She'll know what to do."

"Who is that?"

"Billy Lou."

Jason's brows lifted. "You think she would help me?"

"Of course, she would. Why would you think she wouldn't?"

"I just... I don't know. I just don't want to be a burden on anyone. I mean, I'm already kicking myself for knocking on your door in the middle of the night."

"Never apologize for needing a friend. I'd much rather you knock on my door than face this alone. How do you think you would be doing?" He grimaced and she nodded. "It helps to have others."

"I'm burdening you with my drama, Jamie. I know I am. And that is something I'm ashamed to be doing. I just didn't know what else to do or who else to go to. You were the first person to pop into my mind and I was here banging on your door before I realized what time it was and what I was doing. I'm sorry if I scared you."

"Apology accepted." She stood to her feet, and he grabbed her hand.

"Where are you going?"

She gave it a reassuring squeeze. "I'm just going to get you a blanket and pillow. She walked to her entry closet and pulled them out. "You can sleep on the couch tonight. Jarin is fine in my bed. I have a chaise in my bedroom I can sleep on. In the morning, we'll call Billy Lou and see if she can help guide us in what steps to take next."

"Us?"

"You wanted my help, right?"

"Well, yes, but—"

"Then you have it. Try to get some rest. Tomorrow is going to be a long day." Jamie patted his hand one more time before walking to her room. She quietly entered, offered a tiny wave in his direction, and closed the door behind her. She studied the small boy cuddled in her bed and her heart tore at the sadness he would feel tomorrow once he realized his mother was gone. She prayed Jarin would warm up to his new father and that Billy Lou would be able to help them, because Jamie was at a loss. She didn't know what to do. She didn't know how to help. And she wanted more than anything to be able to do both.

"Just pour this cup of milk into the bowl." Jamie's voice drifted softly through the room as Jason slowly stirred to consciousness. "That's right. Good job. Now, we stir. Like this." She used a wooden spoon and then let Jarin take hold and try his best at mixing the batter together. He stood on one of her dining chairs to reach the counter and his tousled hair showed signs of a restful night for him. Jason blinked to adjust his eyes to the bright sun shining through the small apartment. He groaned as his back stretched and he began to stand. Jarin's head quickly popped up from his task as he nervously glanced Jason's direction. Jamie looked up and smiled. "Good morning, sleepy head."

Jason walked towards them, each step causing Jarin's little hands to fumble more and more as the small boy nervously tucked himself closer to Jamie's side. He was scared of him, and Jason attempted a light tone and mood despite the turmoil of the situation. "Morning. You two are up early."

"Not really," Jamie giggled. She motioned towards the clock and Jason's face blanched.

"Nine!" He hurried towards his cell phone and began searching the cushions to find it.

"Don't worry. Your crew is working where they need to be. And they are fed. I texted Ted Rawlins this morning and told him you wouldn't be in today and that if he wanted goodies, he had to come by and pick them up this morning. He did and said he'd see that things run smoothly today for you. Said he would check in at noon with you."

"Ted?" Jason stared at Jamie.

"Was he not a good choice? I figured since he was your second in command that was the safest bet. I also have his wife's number, so I messaged her for it this morning and she shared it with me. I didn't go through your phone or anything. Though I did place it there on the lamp stand."

Baffled, Jason stared.

"Jason?" Jamie looked as if she were preparing for a lashing, and he shook his head to wake up further.

"No, that's fine. That's... good. Thank you."

"No problem."

"But what about your shop?"

"What about it?"

"You normally open at six."

"And it won't hurt Reesa to wait for a cup of coffee. I'm sure she's drifted to the diner by now anyway."

"Jamie—"

"Don't. It's fine. Billy Lou will be here about 9:30. Jarin is helping me make some muffins for her. He's doing a great job," she praised the little boy again, his young eyes looking up at Jason for approval.

Jamie nodded encouragingly at Jason and tilted her head at the boy. Jason cleared his throat. "Good job, buddy." He eased onto a stool and the little boy watched his every move. "Do you remember me from last night?" Jason asked.

The boy nodded.

"And you know who I am?"

"He's probably not going to understand that," Jamie whispered.

"Do you know my name?" asked Jason, rephrasing.

The boy shook his head.

"Well..." Jason looked to Jamie, and she nodded. "I'm your daddy." He struggled over the last word before clearing his throat again and continuing. "Did you know that?"

The boy shook his head again, his eyes looking up at Jamie. She smiled down at him with excitement and nodded.

"You scared?" Jason asked softly.

The boy's bottom lip trembled as he nodded his head. Jamie lightly brushed a hand over his soft hair.

"You don't have to be scared, okay? We're going to take good care of you. Ms. Jamie here, well, she's the nicest person in the world. Did you know that?"

The boy looked up at Jamie and then back to Jason.

"It's the truth. I've yet to meet a better person. And she's going to help us. Are you okay with Ms. Jamie helping us?"

He nodded, his little hands regripping the spoon, his eyes never leaving Jason's face.

"We're glad you're here." Jason's voice broke as he took a step back and turned away from them to gather his emotions. A knock sounded on the door and Jamie waved for him to answer it as she helped Jarin spoon batter into the muffin tin.

"Ms. Billy Lou." His voice was quiet as the pretty, put-together woman reached her arms out and embraced him, flooding him with expensive perfume, mint bubble gum, and enough comfort to erase a few of his fears. She cupped his face. "Mornin', honey. I hear you've got a morning for the record books."

He smirked despite the circumstances, and she winked at him. "We'll get ya sorted. Don't you worry. Now where's that baby?" She walked inside and she clasped her hands. "My, my, my! Somethin' sure smells good!"

Jarin's head popped up as she walked towards him. "Hi darlin'! Are you makin' some muffins?"

Jarin nodded, his eyes soaking in the vibrant woman in front of him in wonder. "Well, I bet they're delicious. I can't wait to eat one." Billy Lou smiled at Jamie and scooted around the counter to give her an encouraging hug. She gently brushed a hand over the toddler's head. "Goodness me, he looks just like you did at that age, Jason."

"I know."

"Let's hope he's half as devious, hm?" Billy Lou mumbled.

Jamie chuckled at Jason's embarrassed expression.

"Now, let me see that letter. You got the folder she left ya?" Billy Lou walked back over to Jason, and he handed her the letter and watched her read it. She shook her head. "That girl..." she sighed. "Selfish people are blind people. And until one thing changes, the other will stay the same. At least she left you his birth certificate." She pored through the folder of documents and pulled out a piece of paper. "You see this?"

"I honestly didn't really get through it all past the birth certificate."

"Bless your heart, of course you didn't." She held up the paper for him to see it. "That girl has signed over her parental rights to you."

His face was blank, and Billy Lou wriggled the paper. "This means that you now have full custody of your son without her interfering now or in the future."

"Why would she do that?"

"She doesn't want him." Billy Lou stated simply, but in a hushed tone so Jarin didn't overhear.

"But why not?" Jason looked at the boy who flashed a quick, faint smile up at Jamie as she did one of her signature dance moves as they slid the muffins into the oven.

"Only the Lord knows." Billy Lou shook her head in sympathy. "That boy is going to need you, honey. Now, I know you aren't ready. None of us ever are, even when we do have the nine months of pregnancy to prepare us. You've had him dropped in your lap and now have to be a daddy, so I know you are probably feeling a little overwhelmed."

"A *little*?" Jason turned to her stunned. "Billy Lou, I'm drownin' here. I have no clue how to raise a child. What if he doesn't like me? What if I screw him up?"

Billy Lou smirked. "Honey, you are one of the hardest workin' men I know. You're charming, polite, and have a decent head on your shoulders. I think you'll do just fine. You'll find help from your friends." She nodded towards Jamie. "And you'll find help from the community. 'It takes a village' is not just a cliché saying, honey. It's the truth. And lucky for you, you have a village."

"You're in that village, right?" he mumbled.

Billy Lou hooted and patted his shoulder. "Of course, I am. And I just love little ones." They watched as Jamie taught Jarin a dance move that involved him wiggling his little hips and jumping in the air. "She's such a doll."

"She truly is," Jason agreed.

Billy Lou looked up at him and squinted. "You be sweet to her."

Jason's cheeks flushed. "Oh, it's not like that, Ms. Billy Lou. I just appreciate her is all. I don't..." He trailed off as Billy Lou fisted her hands on her hips and narrowed her gaze.

"And why not? She's beautiful, bubbly, and vivacious. She has a heart of gold, works just as hard as you, and supports her friends. She's dedicated to this town, much like yourself, and she answers the door after midnight to a crazy man who needs help. Need I go on?"

Jason chuckled. "No ma'am."

"Good. I suggest, Jason Wright, that you look at that girl as more than just your neighborhood barista and start treatin' her like the jewel she is."

"The ruby of Piney," he muttered under his breath.

Billy Lou softened at his remark and nodded. "Yes. Yes, she is. Now, let's get that boy to talkin' to us. By the end of the hour, he will love you."

"I hope so. He's a little scared of me right now."

"Well, of course he is. You're all legs and broad shoulders, deep voice, and nerves. You're rattlin' in your boots. Let's show him the confident Jason Wright everybody knows and loves, shall we?"

Jason grabbed Billy Lou's hand before she walked off and gave it a friendly pat. "Thank you, Ms. Billy Lou."

She patted his cheek. "Don't you even mention it, honey. I just expect you at my house for Sunday evening supper with the rest of the kids from here on out." She pointed a finger at him until he agreed. "Good."

He relinquished her hand, and she walked over to the kitchen area. Jamie glanced up and tilted her head at him. He gave her a thumbs up and she nodded in acceptance. Her small way of checking on him made him smile as he walked towards the island. Jarin's face grew serious as he looked at him.

"Daddy." Billy Lou pointed at Jason. "Is this your daddy?" she asked the little boy.

He looked to Jason for what to say and Jason nodded his head.

Jarin then affirmed it with a nod of his own head.

"Can you say Daddy?" Billy Lou asked.

The boy stared at her for a moment.

"Billy Lou." She pointed at herself. "Jamie." She pointed to Jamie. "Daddy." She pointed at Jason. She repeated the gesture and before she could reach Jason again, the little boy stated "Beewee." Billy Lou placed a hand over her heart and gushed. "Oh yes! I'm Billy. Good job, baby doll. And my goodness, don't you just have the voice of an angel. Can you say it again?"

"Beewee."

"Oh heavens, I think this little doll has just won my heart." Billy Lou chuckled as she pointed to Jamie. "Jamie," she said slowly.

"Damie," he repeated.

"Woo hoo!" Jamie raised a hand and he smiled before giving her a soft high five.

"Daddy." Billy Lou pointed to Jason and the boy hesitated a moment before he quietly muttered "Daddy" under his breath.

"That's right. Daddy." Billy Lou beamed. "He's a fast learner. Now, Jarin, you tell Ms. Billy what you want to do today. You want to go play at the park?"

The little boy's eyes lit up at her suggestion.

"They have swings, slides, seesaws..." Billy Lou explained, and he jumped on his tiptoes and grinned. Jason's heart lifted at the sight. "Maybe your daddy will take us. What do ya say?" Billy Lou looked up at Jason.

"Yep. The park it is," Jason agreed, his eyes looking up to see if Jamie were willing to join them, but she turned to pull the muffins out of the oven.

"You have to eat first. Jarin and I worked too hard on these muffins for you not to." Jamie made quick work of dishing up the muffins, cutting Jarin's in half to let the steam escape and cool faster.

Billy Lou leaned over her muffin and inhaled a deep breath. "My goodness these smell good. Good job, Jarin.

The little boy's shy smile and overly observant eyes scanned the room until landing upon him. He watched as Jason took a bite too. "Mmm mmm mmm! These are amazing! Good job, buddy."

Jarin's smile widened as he took a bite of his own muffin and accepted the glass of milk Jamie set beside him. She tenderly brushed a hand over his hair before enjoying her own breakfast.

"You'll join us, won't you, Jamie?" Jason asked. "At the park?"

"Oh." Her surprised expression and quick aversion of the eyes gave him his answer before she spoke. "I should get some things done around here; maybe open the shop for the second half of the day."

"Right." Jason shook his head. "I forgot I completely derailed your morning."

"You didn't," Jamie assured him. "I mean, you did, but it's totally okay." She fumbled over her words, her cheeks turning rosy as she began to crumble under Billy Lou's watchful gaze. "Honestly," Jamie assured him. "I just need to get some things done."

"No problem." Jason cleared his throat and set his plate on the counter. "I guess it's park time. Ready?" He looked to Jarin, the little boy hesitant to leave Jamie. He looked up at her in silent plea and she gave him an encouraging smile.

"You have fun, Jarin. I can't wait for you to tell me all about it. Okay?"

The boy's eyes glassed over as he realized he'd be leaving her and he nodded, his bottom lip trembling as Jason held out his hand to him. Billy Lou hopped off her stool and grabbed Jarin's other hand. "Don't you forget about me now. I love to swing. And I bet your daddy can push us *real* high." She patted his small hand until he managed a watery smile.

Jason stopped at the door as Billy Lou could be heard talking in upbeat tones to his son on the way down the stairs. He paused and watched Jamie start to straighten up her kitchen. "Thank you, Jamie. Again. For everything."

She glanced up, her easy smile at the ready. He took a step towards her and then paused, realizing he'd wanted to walk back to her kitchen and pull her close. "Don't mention it," she replied. "Maybe we can meet up for supper later."

"Yes." He readily agreed, relief washing over him knowing he'd have her help once again. He also felt a small lift in his chest at having the opportunity of spending more time with her. "But at my place. What d'ya say?"

"Oh." Surprise had Jamie considering. "Alright. Do I need to bring anything?"

"Nope. Allow me to feed you for once." Jason grinned. "Though it probably won't be as good as your cookin'."

Jamie chuckled. "Don't be so hard on yourself. The only people that can out-cook me are Billy Lou and T.J., though don't tell him I said that. He'd never let me live it down."

"My lips are sealed." Jason sighed as he walked back to the doorway. "I'm a little scared to walk out of here. I mean... in here I can just be me. Out there... it's all new territory for me."

"You're a fast learner," Jamie encouraged, walking towards him to aid in nudging him out of her house. "He's a sweet kid. Shy. But I think that's just because he's completely surrounded by new faces. I have a feeling he'll start perking up the next couple of days." Jamie smiled up at him. "He has your eyes."

Jason rubbed a hand over the back of his neck and nodded. "I noticed that too."

"Go. Have fun. Be fun. And I will see you two guys later, okay?"

Jason reached for her hand and held it a moment, looking down at her perfectly trimmed nails. She didn't waste time or money on polish, Jamie was just sensible. But her hands were soft and strong. He lifted one to his lips and kissed the back of it. "Thank you." He released his hold and walked out into the morning sun to a chattering Billy Lou and timid little boy.

CHAPTER EIGHT

She didn't open up her store. She was too tired to even think about mixing coffees. And that was okay, because clearly, Reesa clearly needed her. She watched as her friend frantically rushed about her small cabin, rearranging furniture, fluffing pillows, moving frames all in a frenzy. "No, no, no... maybe the couch should stay where it was, and I will move the chair. What do you think?" Reesa looked up and Jamie sighed.

"I think you are stressing over this too much. Your mom isn't going to care where your couch sits."

"Wrong!" Reesa stated. "She most certainly will. She'll look about the room with disdain and then silently judge me for every decorative decision."

"And I think you're wrong. I doubt she even expects you to let her in the door, so I imagine she will enjoy the few minutes she's given to take a peek at the life you've created with Clare."

Reesa paused in her movements, Jamie's words sinking in. "You think she'll be that observant?"

"Yes. After watching her with Clare the other day, I think she will be quiet, collected, and soaking in the time she has with the both of you."

Reesa ran a hand through her hair and puffed a relieved breath. "You're probably right. I shouldn't assume she's going to act the monster. That's wrong of me. Even if it's been my experience, it's wrong of me to not at least give her the benefit of the doubt... cautiously." Jamie smiled in agreement. "I'm glad you'll be stopping by to relieve what I know will be thick tension."

"Oh, right." Jamie grimaced. "About that..."

Reesa's eyes rounded. "Don't say you're backing out on me."

"Well..."

"What? No!" Reesa clasped her hands together and danced from foot to foot. "Why?"

"Jason needs help."

"With what? His ex still in town?"

Jamie shook her head. "It's actually what I came to talk to you about." Jamie relaxed in one of Reesa's deep-set chairs, the crocheted granny square pillow snug under her arm. "She left."

"Is that not a good thing?" Reesa asked. "He didn't seem like he wanted to see her. I mean, I hope they worked something out regarding his son, but..."

"No. She left in the middle of the night and left Jarin, the boy, with Jason."

The seriousness of turn in the conversation had Reesa slowly sinking to a sitting position on her couch as she quietly soaked in the information. "Wow."

"Yeah. He showed up at my place around one this morning in a complete panic." Jamie gave Reesa the complete rundown, including the help that Billy Lou was providing today. "So, I came here this afternoon because I'm exhausted and not really in the mood to open the shop, but he's asked me over for dinner later this evening. Jarin has taken a shine to me."

"Of course, he has. You're awesome," Reesa complimented. "Wow. Poor Jason. I know he was shocked to find out he had a son, but for her to just leave the poor boy... that's tough."

"Yeah."

Reesa's brows lifted slightly. "Although, I do find it *quite* interesting that Jason drives to your house in the middle of the night for help. Thoughts on that?" Her sly smirk told Jamie the matchmaking wheels were turning.

"Probably because I'd just seen him. I was just the person on his mind, I'm sure."

"I bet you were," Reesa muttered and then grinned.

"It's not like that." Jamie rolled her eyes. "Jason doesn't see me as more than a friend, Reesa. Trust me. He never has and he never will."

"Would you want him to?" Reesa asked.

Sighing, Jamie rubbed a loose strand of yarn in between her fingers on top of the pillow, avoiding her friend's stare. "I've thought about it, but it's just not in the cards. Never has been. Jason's always gone after the beautiful bombshells."

"Um, you're a beautiful bombshell," Reesa pointed out.

Jamie chuckled. "Thanks for that, but you know what I mean."

"No, I don't," Reesa countered. "You are beautiful, Jamie. And even better, not only are you beautiful on the outside, you're beautiful on the inside. Do you know how rare that is?"

Emotion swelled in Jamie's eyes at her friend's words, Reesa fixing her with a hard gaze. "I don't know why you can't see it. Sure, you may not have been Miss Popular in high school, but just because you weren't, that doesn't mean you weren't pretty or worth a guy's time. Theo has always thought the world of you."

"As a friend," Jamie pointed out. "Though, I've never wanted more than that with Theo, just so you know," she clarified.

Reesa smiled in understanding. "All I'm saying is that you need to give yourself more credit. You're gorgeous with that red hair and those bright blue eyes. You have the body of a goddess," Reesa waved a hand over her. "And you have the heart so kind and so rare, that the right man is out there for you, and he's dreaming of you at this very moment."

Jamie felt a tear slide down her cheek and exhaled a shaky breath. "Whoa."

"I'm a mom of a teenage girl; I'm good at these kinds of talks. But I mean every single word. Stop believing 'a man like Jason' wouldn't want you. He'd be lucky to have you. In my eyes, he's the one who would need to step up his game to deserve you."

"Well, I don't think his game is on his mind at the moment, even if I do have the body of a goddess." Jamie giggled at that description. She'd never considered her plump figure an asset. If anything, she'd been more self-conscious about her weight over the years than any other aspect of herself. She hated that she was, that she caved into the societal pressures of being thin and that she let it infiltrate her thoughts at times. Overall, though, she was happy with herself, her life, and even her figure. She just sometimes simply stumbled into that ridiculous societal mindset. But she also knew that even if she was happy with her looks and stature, she wasn't the typical 'type' Jason seemed to float around with, or marry, for that matter.

"Seriously, Jamie, do you have feelings for Jason?" Reesa asked curiously.

"I think I might," Jamie admitted. "I'm trying not to, but it's been nice to get to know him better. To see underneath the public visage he portrays. He's not some womanizer that everyone thinks he is, which was nice to discover. And he's genuinely one of the nicest men in Piney."

"Dang it," Reesa murmured. "Now you're making me like him more." She sighed and leaned back into her cushions. "I think he's a good guy too," Reesa admitted. "And if you think he is worth your time and energy and affection, then I stand with you. But if he does anything to hurt you, he's blacklisted forever."

Jamie giggled. "Well, he doesn't even know I have feelings for him, so let's just keep that on the downlow. It won't amount to anything, and right now I just want to be a good friend. That's what he needs."

"Right. It's hard single parenting."

"I don't know how you did it at such a young age." Jamie eyed her friend. "And I know with your mom coming later you're probably feeling like that teenager all over again."

"Yes." Reesa shook her head in disappointment. "I don't know why, but I do. I feel like that scared, nervous, disappointing teenager she more than likely remembers. And I know I'm not, but for some reason that's where my mind keeps going."

"Do I need to give you the pep talk now?"

Laughing, Reesa shook her head. "No, I think I'm good. "I keep telling Clare that tonight is all about her getting to know her grandmother, not about me, so I'll just keep throwing her to the wolves when things get dicey."

"Such a noble thing to do," Jamie teased.

"Meh, she's a teenager. They're made of firmer stuff than we are."

"Not to mention, if your mother decides to bare her own claws, T.J. will go full on bear mode to protect the two of you."

"There is that." Reesa smiled tenderly. "I know it will be fine this evening. I do. Dad has worked really hard at making an effort with Clare, and even in connecting with me. He likes Theo and seems to be enjoying fitting into the mix now. Let's hope my mom won't disrupt that, but will enjoy it too."

"I think she will," Jamie assured her. "The way she stared at Clare the other day, you could tell her heart was just devastated at not knowing her."

Reesa cleared her throat and hopped to her feet before a melancholy mood fell through the room again. "Well, enough of all that. You have a hot date tonight. We should be excited about that."

"Whoa, whoa, whoa," Jamie chuckled. "It's not a date. It's a 'help me!' meal."

"Tomato, to-mahto." Reesa smirked. "So, what are you going to wear?"

"What I have on." Jamie waved a hand over her jeans and button-up top. Reesa shook her head.

"Girl, no. You need to wear a dress. Show off that gorgeous figure."

"I'm not going to flirt and show off tonight, Reesa. I'm going to help ease and comfort a friend and his little boy."

"Yes, but also to let Jason see not only how amazing you are at being a friend, but also how beautimous you are." She winked. "You should wear that sundress you have— that long maxi dress. It hugs in all the right places. It's a great color on you. And with some cute earrings—" She reached up and removed the studs from her own ears and held them out to Jamie. "You're all set."

"You are too much sometimes."

"Don't I know it." Theo's voice had both women jumping as he walked from the back of the house.

"Geez, T.J., you gave me a heart attack."

"What are you doing here?" Reesa asked, standing on her tiptoes to kiss his cheek. "And sneaking in the back door at that?"

"Brought over a new water bowl for Trooper and set it up back there." Theo motioned over his shoulder. "And it's lunch time, so I thought I might sneak a sandwich off of you."

"I'm not sure I have anything in the fridge." Reesa watched as he walked over and helped himself to new groceries that had somehow made their way into her refrigerator. "You're good."

He smirked over his shoulder and Jamie stood. "I should be heading out."

"Don't leave on my account." Theo stood, sandwich makings in his large hands.

"I'm not. I need to go grab a nap before this evening."

"Oh right, you still coming later?" he asked.

"No, she has a date." Reesa wriggled her eyebrows.

Jamie tossed the chair pillow at her and rolled her eyes before meeting Theo's concerned gaze. "It's not a date. I'm helping Jason with his son."

"Right. Grandma texted me about that earlier." Theo set his ingredients on the counter and began making two sandwiches. "You let me know if he needs any help. Not sure what I could do, but..."

"I know." Jamie smiled. "We're here for him. That's what I'm going to make sure he understands. He's not in this transition alone."

"You Piney people." Reesa fanned a hand over her face to dry her glassy eyes. "Changing lives and loving people like it's nothing."

"The right people are easy to love." Theo hugged her to his side and then winked at Jamie.

"I'll keep you two posted. Ya'll just keep on being adorable." She giggled as she walked to the door and stepped out onto the porch.
"Wear the sundress!" Reesa called after her.

Laughing, Jamie just bent down to pet an awaiting Trooper before walking to her car. Perhaps she might wear that dress. Perhaps she might.

^

Jamie pulled to a stop outside of Jason's house and he sat on the bottom step of his front porch at ease as he listened to a departing Billy Lou give him instructions. He glanced up as Jamie rounded the front of her car, the bright turquoise dress and that tumbling red hair causing his ears to ring and drown out the kind Billy Lou. The woman followed his gaze and stopped mid-sentence. "Well," Billy Lou beamed. "Hi, honey. Don't you look just beautiful! Doesn't she, Jason?"

Jamie blushed at the compliment and waved it away. "I had a day off and took the liberty of wearing more than jeans and coffee stains, that's all."

"You should do it more often." Billy Lou nodded her approval and then stifled a smile at Jason's stunned expression as he continued watching Jamie. She lightly kicked his boot and he blinked, clambering to his feet and brushing his hands over his jeans.

"You came." Jason's fumbling response had Billy Lou stifling a chuckle as she lightly rested a hand on his shoulder.
"You call me if you need me." She lightly patted Jamie's arm on her way to her car and Jamie nodded towards the house.

"Is Jarin acclimating well?"

"Oh, right, yes. Sort of. I think so." Jason admired her from behind as she walked up his front porch steps and collected himself before treading after her. "He's watching some sort of kid show right now. Billy Lou said he could, so..."

Jamie smirked at that and the little boy looked up when she walked in. She waved enthusiastically, his small, serious face splitting into a welcoming smile. "What'cha watchin'?" He pointed to the screen and she nodded. "That's a great show. You like it?" He nodded again and went back to the animated creatures on the screen. "How was the park?" Jamie asked, turning to face him.

"It was good." He motioned her towards the kitchen and she followed him to the small room tucked off the living room. She found a seat at a small dinette table, the wooden surface scarred from years of use, but beautiful and smooth to the touch. He stirred something on top of the stovetop, the smell telling her it was some sort of vegetable. "He opened up a bit. Calls me Daddy now, which, if I'm honest, feels amazing." He held a hand over his heart, and she smiled at him.

"See, you're already a natural."

"I wouldn't go that far." Jason beamed. "Billy Lou was a Godsend. She kept him moving and playing. They wore me out. But we went for ice cream and then he napped for a bit, which Billy Lou said was important at his age, and then he woke up a bit ago. She said toys and a little tv would satisfy him until supper. He's played with a few old cars I had lying around from when I was a kid. I definitely need to buy him some toys."

"That will come. And everyone else will buy him toys, and pretty soon you'll be wishing you didn't have so many under your feet. You don't have to jump into a thousand toys at once."

"That's what Billy Lou said." Jason nodded. "And I get it. I do. But now that he seems to be warming up to the house and me, I want him to pick out a few tomorrow, though I'm not sure when I'll take him. After work, I guess. Billy Lou said she'd watch him for me during work hours until I find a sitter or figure out a better situation. I'm swamped right now with projects, so it's a bit of a... I don't want to say hassle, but it's a hiccup in my routine that I've got to figure out. A good hiccup, don't get me wrong, but a hiccup," he babbled. He could feel it. His nerves from the day, his excitement over Jarin clicking with him, Jamie in that dress. He felt the nervous energy bubbling forth of its own volition and he paused a moment to let his heart ease back into its normal rhythm. When he glanced her way, it leapt onward as if he had no control over its pace. And to be honest, he really didn't. "You're gorgeous." The words slipped out and he blanched at the fact they did before he coughed into his fist and cleared his throat. "I mean, you look gorgeous tonight."

Her smile radiated through the room, and he felt short of breath. "Thank you."

He soaked in the image of her sitting at his table and then pointed to the stove. "I've got sauteed veggies, beef stir fry, and if you're lucky, mac and cheese." He flushed at that one. "Billy Lou said I needed a backup plan just in case Jarin is a picky eater."

"Wise woman." Jamie grinned. "That all sounds amazing. Can I help with anything?"

"Nope. I—" He held up a finger and rushed to a small cabinet off the living room and formal dining area and came back carrying two wine glasses. He held one up and she nodded. He made quick work of the cork and poured a glass of deep red wine for her. When he set it on the table, his hand slightly shook. What was wrong with him? He rubbed his sweaty palm down his pant leg and sat across from her. "Only needs a couple more minutes."

She took a sip of the wine and nodded. "That's nice after today."

"Bad day?"

"Not at all, actually. A relaxing one. I haven't taken a day off in I don't know how long, and today I did. I visited with Reesa. I wore comfy clothes all day. I napped. It's been a good day."

"I'm glad. You deserve it." Jason took a sip of his own drink and observed her over the rim. She seemed at ease, though also slightly jittery at his attention. "I'm sorry, again, for banging on your door so early this morning."

"You're forgiven. It was for a good cause."

"Yeah..." He leaned so he could peer around the doorway and checked on Jarin. The boy ran his old toy car over the edge of the coffee table as his eyes darted between car and television screen. "He's pretty great. Laid back. He's cried a couple of times today, just missing Janessa, but overall, he's been pretty chill. I'm sure when it sets in that she's not coming back we'll have some hard days, but he seems okay so far. Sweet kid."

"That's good. He looks so much like you."

"I know, right?" Jason smirked. "Poor kid."

Jamie rolled her eyes in response and Jason felt his own neck heat at the soft compliment. He reached across the table and grabbed her hand, and she eyed him curiously. He brushed his thumb over the top of her knuckles in a soft, circular motion. "Listen, Red..." He glanced up at her and she held a serious expression, her blue eyes so focused upon his face he felt as if he'd turn to mush if he didn't look away soon. "I don't want you worrying about breakfast for my crew tomorrow morning. It's Saturday and I know that's one of your busiest days at the coffee shop. I don't want you to have to worry about my team when I've disrupted your week enough already."

"I don't mind." She slipped her hand away from his touch and back to her wine glass stem, and he found he missed the contact. "It's part of my day anyway. If you want to still provide your team with food, I can do it."

"I know you can do it. I just... I don't want to be any more of a burden than I already have been this week."

"You're not a burden. One, it's my job and I love the extra income. That's how a business grows. Two, you're my friend. It's not considered helping if it's a friend. It's just seeing about one another. And I don't mind either one of those things."

His lips tilted into a lopsided smile as he studied her genuine expression. "Alright, I guess that settles it, then. Breakfast for the crew tomorrow morning."

She nodded and then sniffed the air. "I think our supper is finished."

He jumped to his feet and dread filled his gut. "No. No, no, no, no, no." He lifted the lid on his stir-fry and a plume of smoke lifted into the air. A few seconds later the smoke detector started chiming. "Ah, man!" Jason grabbed a hand towel and began waving it in the air beneath the detector. Jamie turned to a wide-eyed Jarin and motioned for him to come sit with her while Jason rushed around the kitchen and opened windows. The alarm finally quieted, and Jason fisted his hands on his hips. "Well, that was supper." He tossed the kitchen towel onto the counter in frustration and lifted the lid on the mac and cheese. "At least one thing is edible."

Jamie giggled and then a full-blown laugh escaped her lips, and she snuggled Jarin into her arms as he giggled too. "Daddy buuurn," he said.

"Yes, yes he did." Jamie tickled Jarin's ribs before releasing him to run back into the living room.

Jason's regret softened into a lazy smile as he rubbed a hand over his tired face. "Alright, so I'm not a Jamie Bishop in the kitchen. You caught me."

She held up her hands as she stood to her feet. She walked over to his refrigerator and opened the door to empty shelves, save a half carton of milk and a stick of butter that graced them. She tsked her tongue and then walked over to the walk-in pantry. "Dismal, Jason Wright. Just dismal."

He closed his eyes and covered his face in his hands before lowering them to find her standing directly in front of him, her blue eyes dancing in amusement. "I'm not finding this as funny as you," he mumbled miserably.

She grasped his hands in hers and gave them an encouraging squeeze. "I'm sorry. I don't find it funny. Well, sort of. I appreciate you going to all the trouble of cooking, but I think we should all go to the store and find something to make together. It's still early enough, and he doesn't seem overly hungry yet. We'll make an adventure out of it."

He continued gripping her hands and lifted them up to his face. He kissed the backs of her knuckles on both hands. "No."

Her face fell slightly before a wall erected over her emotions and she started to step back. He didn't release her hands. Instead, he pulled her to him and wrapped his arms around her. She stiffened before he tightened the embrace and slowly her body relaxed against his. Her head fit perfectly right beneath his chin, and he rested his cheek on top of her glorious red hair. He felt her lightly tap his back and he pulled back just enough to peer down at her upturned face. "You okay?" she asked.

Inches. Inches between them and he wanted to… he wanted to brush his lips against hers and sample the sweetness of Jamie Bishop. But he couldn't. She was too precious to him. He wouldn't jeopardize their friendship over what he knew he would fail at in the long run—a relationship. So, instead of caving into the feelings he'd had brewing over the last couple of weeks, he eased his hold on her. "I am now. I just... needed that."

She smiled. "Well, since you shot down my grocery idea, what's your plan?"

"I didn't shoot down your idea."

"Yes, you did. You said no."

"Well, yeah, I meant right then. I needed a hug first. I'm good now. Centered." He nodded an affirmative to the fact and he grinned. "Now, I can face the grocery store."

She chuckled. "You're a mess. Come on." She walked into the living room and clapped her hands. "Come on, Jarin. We're going shopping."

The little boy smiled and ran to Jason as he helped him put on his shoes. "I take car?" He held up the vintage toy and Jason nodded. Jason stood to his feet and stopped short as Jarin slid his small hand in his own to head out the door. The small act nearly undid him, and he caught Jamie's pleased expression as well.

"Alright, Jarin. It's up to us to treat Ms. Jamie to a fun time. You think we can have fun?"

"Yes!" He jumped in excitement. "I wike fun!"

"Me too!" Jamie cheered behind them as they walked out. Jason slipped Jarin into his brand new car seat, courtesy of Billy Lou, and buckled him in. Jamie hopped into his front passenger seat and snapped her own seatbelt into place. The ease with which she jumped right into the swing of things was an underestimated skill. He reached across to her, his palm up. She glanced at it a moment before placing her hand in his. He gave it a friendly squeeze before releasing it to turn the key.

"Off we go then." He cranked the engine, smiled in the rearview mirror at his son and then pulled out of the driveway and headed towards town.

CHAPTER NINE

Her cell phone rang and Jamie answered on the second ring. "What's wrong?" she asked immediately.

Reesa's voice flooded the line in a panic. "I can't do this, Jamie. I can't do this. They just pulled up. My dad *and* my mom. They're both here." A sob escaped her best friend's lips and she could hear all the years of Reesa's abandonment and hurt echoing through the phone.

"Calm down. Take a deep breath, Reesa. You're going to be okay. Remember how loved you are? Remember we talked about how wonderful your life is, and how your mom is going to love you and Clare once she gets to know you guys. This is a great step."

"Theo's meeting them outside. I needed a minute."

Jason glanced in Jamie's direction with concern. "Do I need to drop you off?" he whispered.

Jamie shook her head. "Reesa, stop panicking or you're going to make Clare nervous."

"She's in her room. She hasn't seen me like this."

"Good."

"I think... I think it's just me. I think I'm the only one having a hard time with this. Theo seems fine. Clare seems fine. My dad has a smile on his face. My mom even has a placid smile on, though hers could be fake. She was always good at those. Ugh, see? I'm already doing it! I'm already judging every single action she takes, and she's going to do the same."

"No. Calm down. She won't. She's on your turf. You set the tone. And blubbering and being spiteful is not the tone you want to set." Jamie's voice hardened into a scold, and she continued. "Now, you go to your bathroom, splash some water on your face, reapply that mascara, and you march your cute butt out there and you master the art of fake smiling. Fake it 'til you make it, kid."

"Geez, you sure know how to ruin a good fit throwing."

Jamie chuckled. "That's why you called me."

"You're right. I can do this. I'm awesome." Reesa sniffed back her tears.

"You are awesome. Glad you remember. Now, go have a good dinner."

"Dinner," Reesa reminded herself. "Oh, right. How's your dinner going with Mr. Wright?" Her leading tone had Jamie blushing.

"Fine. We're headed into town."

"Oh really?" Reesa continued.

"Yes. Now, go. Your company is at your house. Stop stalling. Bye." Jamie hung up before Reesa could mutter another word.

"Wow. You're tough." Jason smirked as he pulled into the parking lot of the grocery store. "Reesa okay?"

"Not really, but she will be. I was supposed to stop by later to help ease the tension, but—"

"Do you need to? I don't mind. I don't want to take up your entire evening if you have other plans too."

"No, no it's fine. I chose this plan. I want to be with you." She blushed quickly to amend her words. "Guys. *You guys*," she added.

He acknowledged the slip up with a small smirk but didn't flirt further,r for which she was grateful. No telling what else she might say with her nerves so jumpy. He reached across the console and squeezed her hand. "I'm glad you did." He held her eyes for a moment before turning to the back seat to face his son. "Ready, Freddie?"

"I not Fweddie. I Jawin."

Jason winked at him. "Oh, right. Jarin. You look like a Freddie."

Jarin giggled and Jamie smiled at the pure, childish delight in the boy as Jason opened his door to pick him up out of his seat. Jason carried him easily in his left arm, the little boy draping a casual arm around his dad's neck. Jamie knew she had to paint that image one day. Jason had no idea how easy he made this transition look. He was a natural with Jarin, and the boy seemed to love him already. She paused a moment and said, "Hey, you two." They turned and she held an imaginary camera. "Smile." They both flashed cheesy grins— the same grin, she realized— and her heart melted at the sight. She pretended to take their picture. "That's one for the books, for sure."

Jason nudged her with his elbow as she chuckled. When they entered the grocery store, Jarin agreed to sit in the front of the cart so he could kick his legs. "Well, what's your fancy, Ms. Jamie?" Jason asked.

"Hmmm... what pairs well with mac and cheese?"

"Hot dog!" Jarin yelled.

Jason's brows lifted. "A hot dog? You want to treat Ms. Jamie to a fancy dinner, and you choose a hot dog?"

The boy bounced in his seat and nodded. "Hot dog."

Jamie giggled. "I could go for a hot dog."

"Alright," Jason steered their cart down the aisle towards the refrigerated section. "Hot dogs it is."

"Yay!" Jarin cheered. "I eat two hot dogs."

"Two?!" Jason's eyes widened. "You're just pullin' my leg. You're too little to eat two."

"No, I not." Jarin replied. "I big."

"Are you?" Jason held a hand above Jarin's head and then pretended to measure the boys' height while sitting in the cart to a standing Jamie. He lifted his hand as if the boy soared past her. "You're right. You are big. Two hot dogs coming up."

Jarin beamed.

Jason guided the cart around the corner of the aisle and halted when he lightly bumped the end of his cart into someone.

"Ugh, watch it!" A teenage voice shrilled as a young blond spun with fury in her eyes.

Jason grimaced. "Sorry about that."

She tossed her hair over her shoulder and spun away from him as an embarrassed teenage boy looked up at them. Teddy Graham.

"Teddy," Jamie greeted, her eyes darting to the girl. "How've you been?"

"Hi, Ms. Jamie. Mr. Wright. Been good. Who's this?" He pointed to Jarin and Jason stood up straight and proud.

"This is my son, Jarin. He's new in town."

Teddy's eyes widened in surprise. "Wow. Cool. He looks just like you."

"Handsome, you mean." Jason smirked as Jamie elbowed him.

"We've missed seeing you around," Jamie continued. "Charlie and Clare finished her truck."

Teddy's cheeks reddened and he shyly replied. "Yeah, I saw her drive it to school the other day. It looks good."

"Teddy, come on, let's go." The girl tugged on his arm and he flashed an apologetic gaze in Jamie's direction.

"Guess I'll see you around," Teddy mumbled, his footsteps hesitant as the girl continued to tug him further down the aisle and away from them and conversation about Clare. "Tell Clare—" He paused, the girl's eyes flashing furiously before he continued. "Nice truck."

Jamie smiled and nodded. "I will."

"You two have fun. No shenanigans. My chickens prefer a peaceful night's sleep." Jason pointed at him and Teddy blushed as the girl cackled in a surprisingly awful laugh as they walked away. "Wow." Jason pretended to rub his ear and Jamie snorted back a laugh.

"Come on, you goober."

"Poor guy is roped in tight."

"He'll wise up. You can tell he's miserable. He just needs to man up." Jamie glanced over at the hot dogs, grabbed a package, and handed them to Jarin. He tossed them over his shoulder to land in the basket portion of the cart and smiled. She high fived him for the teamwork.

"I don't know if he will. He seems to be in pretty deep." Jason held up a bag of shredded cheese and Jamie and Jarin both nodded. He grinned as he handed it to Jarin to toss over his shoulder into the basket.

They navigated around the grocery store and filled the cart to brimming. At the checkout, Jarin handed several items to Jason as he placed them on the conveyor belt and the cashier scanned their items. "This should last us what, two weeks?"

Jamie laughed. "I would sure hope so. You two definitely won't go hungry. I'm bummed, though." She held up a muffin mix. "Guess I won't be seeing you two show up at my door for these anymore."

"Those are just a mix. Yours are way better than those," Jason replied. "Besides, I'll probably burn them anyway."

"Have faith in your abilities." She smiled. "But you two have to stop by every now and then and let him help me in the kitchen. He seemed to like that."

Jason nodded. "I think he would. I would too, if you don't mind me tagging along."

"Of course not." She watched as he slid his debit card through the machine and paid for the groceries. She loaded Jarin into his car seat as Jason stacked groceries on the other side of the back seat. Jarin chattered away about mac and cheese and hot dogs, Jamie giving cheerful words in response. She looked up to find Jason watching her. She snapped the last of Jarin's buckles and handed him his toy car before closing his door and walking to the other side. She handed a few remaining bags to Jason, their fingers tangling together in the handles. Jason used his free hand to work the bag free and placed them in the back with the others. He shut the door and then beat Jamie's hand to the handle of her own. "Oh," She flushed. "Why thank you, Mr. Wright."

His devastating smile flashed as he leaned close to her. "My pleasure, Ms. Bishop." He lingered a moment, the smell of his cologne sending her pulse into overdrive. His eyes darted down to her lips a brief second before he stepped away and shut her door. She heaved a heavy sigh before he climbed behind the wheel.

The drive back to his house was quiet, other than Jarin's ramblings in the back seat. Jamie was unsure what to say after the flirtatious moment leaving the store. Had there been a moment? Yes, she was sure of it. There had most definitely been a moment... right? She was grateful when he pulled to a stop in front of his house, and she could open the truck door and breathe in some fresh air. She began gathering groceries as Jason helped Jarin out of the car and the little boy ran up the front porch steps. She unbagged various items as Jason continued making treks out to his truck, relishing having the space to herself for a moment. When he returned, he began putting items away, only leaving out the makings for hot dogs. "Guess we'll have to heat up the mac and cheese again, or do you think it's ruined?" He lifted the lid and peered inside the pot. Jamie leaned over and looked.

"It looks fine. We can turn it on low." She turned the knob to the stove top and began prepping hot dogs. "Boil the dogs or grill?"

"I didn't even know you could boil hot dogs." Jason looked perplexed. "That kind of sounds gross, so I will just fire up the grill."

She smiled as she set the tray aside and watched him go outside to situate the fire for the grilling. Her phone dinged and Reesa texted a picture of her mother sitting with Clare, the two of

them looking through some sort of photo album. Her heart ached for her friend, knowing what a bittersweet moment that must be for her to witness. Jamie sent a swift text back:
"Memories in the making." She pocketed her phone as Jason walked back inside.

"Reesa, again?" he asked.

"Yeah. It seems to be going okay with her parents."

"That's good." He watched as she opened a cabinet, and didn't find what she was looking for, and opened another one.

"Plates?" she asked.

He walked towards her and opened the next cabinet in line. "Ah." She reached into the cabinet and grabbed three and set them on the counter. "You—" She paused as he twirled one of her stray curls around his finger and slid closer to her.

"You have the silkiest hair." His voice was barely audible as he eyed his hand and her hair in wonder. "I've always wondered what your curls would feel like."

Surprised by that revelation, Jamie dared to meet his eyes. "Really?"

He nodded as a slow smile spread over his lips. "Once in tenth grade, you sat in front of me for Chemistry class. I wanted to tug on these curls all the time. One time I slipped my pencil through one of the loops. You didn't notice. Theo did, though. I remember the irritated frown he cast my way." He smirked at the memory as his other hand gently lifted to cup her cheek, his thumb brushing over the faint dusting of freckles. Her heart tightened in her chest at the tenderness. Jason Wright was— She shifted away and busied her hands at the counter, breaking the contact. There was no way Jason was about to kiss her. He was just caught up in the moment, or something. He didn't move when she pulled away. Instead, he shifted closer to her each time she shuffled away.

"You're going to run out of room here soon, Red. You only have to tell me no. And if I've misread things between us lately, then forgive me for making you feel awkward."

"Awkward? I'm not awkward," she fumbled.

He laughed as her nervous hands squirted too much mustard on a hot dog bun and it splattered the counter. Her cheeks flushed as she ripped a paper towel off the roll and quickly cleaned up the mess. He snatched the paper towel from her fingers and she jumped. "Come on now, Jamie."

"Alright, you're making me nervous."

"I'm making you nervous?"

"Yes."

"Why?"

"Because you're... just being... you."

"Is that an insult? Or a good thing?" Jason asked.

"It's good. Fine. Totally fine. I just— why?"

"Why, what?"

"Why are you being..." She wasn't quite sure how to finish her question.

"Why do I want to kiss you?" he finished, unashamed of sharing his current goal.

Her heart hammered against her ribs.

"Well, for starters, you look awfully pretty tonight." He took a step closer to her. "Second, you have the silkiest hair I've ever felt or seen. Third, you smell good." He leaned towards her and inhaled, his hand lightly resting against her hip as he tugged her close. "Fourth, I've rather liked getting to know you better. Fifth," he continued. "You have a beautiful heart." He kissed her forehead, and she held back a shudder as his lips lightly grazed their way down the bridge of her nose. "Sixth," he whispered, lightly kissing the tip of her nose, "I think you're the best person I've ever known. And all that wraps up into a beautiful," He kissed her left cheek, his free hand sliding up her back to rest behind her neck, his fingers lightly toying with her hair as he went. "Gorgeous, generous, genuine package that I find quite irresistible." He kissed her right cheek. "Am I overstepping?" he whispered, pulling back just enough to gaze into what she knew were terrified eyes. She watched him study her a moment. Regret flashed across his face before he lowered his forehead to hers. He pulled away on an apology. "I'm sorry. I can tell I've misread things. You look like a deer caught in the headlights. I understand." He backed completely away, his hands slipping from her body, and she immediately missed them. "I'm sorry. It won't happen again, Red. Please don't let this ruin things between us. I value you as a friend." He turned to walk outside to check the grill.

Jamie inhaled a panicked breath, her heart bound to leap right out of her chest. She peeked her head around the corner of the kitchen to make sure Jarin was watching his show on the television. The young boy was happy as could be. Jason had wanted to kiss her. Her panic had nothing to do with not caring for him or wanting him to. She was just surprised. Jason Wright... *Jason Wright* liked *her*! Her cheeks flushed at the thought, and she hurried outside to where he stood at the grill. He closed the hot dogs inside to cook and turned just as she reached him. She grabbed the tray from his hands and set it on the rail of his deck before throwing her arms around his neck and claiming his mouth with hers. He stumbled a step but quickly reclaimed his footing as his mouth took the lead and he wound his hands into her hair. Her hands gripped the front of his shirt as she tugged him closer, and they bumped into the back door as he pinned her there, his hands cupping her face as they melted into one another.

^

Jason loved the feel of Jamie in his arms, her scent wrapping around him, her warmth, her passion. He lost himself in her, his hands continually finding their way into her glorious mass of red curls. He withdrew a moment, and she opened her eyes, concern already blooming there at what they'd just done. That they'd both just tumbled off the ledge from friendship into something more. Before she could shyly back away, he gently slid his hands to her wrists. "Don't sneak away. I just…" He nodded towards the grill. "I've already burned one supper tonight. I don't want to make it two."

She grinned, a soft chuckle escaping her lips as she nodded and watched him retrieve the hot dogs. They carried them inside and she made a plate for Jarin, calling him to the table. The little boy sat joyfully in a seat and began munching away, his appetite in full force. Jason ruffled a hand over his hair and then looked up at Jamie. Her cheeks were still flushed and her hair somewhat jumbled, but she was beautiful. He smiled at her as he motioned towards the food. "Your feast, my precious ruby."

She exaggerated a fluffing hand to her hair in pure Jamie Bishop fashion as she chuckled. "I love hot dogs." She looked to Jarin, and he nodded in agreement.

"Hot dog yummy to my tummy."

Jason and Jamie exchanged amused glances with one another at his expression. He ate quickly, devouring his designated two hot dogs and two helpings of mac and cheese before Jason deemed him worthy of a bubble bath. Jarin liked the sound of that and already seemed to know his way to the bathroom down the hall. Jason held up a finger to Jamie. "Be right back."

"Take your time. I'll clean up." She stood and gathered their plates.

She could hear Jarin's squeals as water began filling the tub, as well as bubbles, from the sound of his delight. She smiled to herself as she listened to Jason talking with his son, the ease with which he slid into the role sweet and tender. They had rough days ahead, she knew, but he seemed to be catching on quickly. He walked into the kitchen and watched her for a moment. "Billy Lou hooked me up with diapers, pull-ups, and bubble bath. All three have come in handy. I'm a bit clumsy with the diaper gig, but pull-ups are easy enough, so we've burned through quite a bit of those today."

She grinned. "Yay for potty training soon."

"Um, yeah... not exactly something I'm prepared for."

"You're handling it like a professional. You're a natural."

"Well, one day at a time." Jason watched as she dried the plates and put them back in the cabinet. "Listen, Jamie—"

She held up a hand. "You don't have to say it. I get it. You've been under a lot of stress lately and your emotions got the best of you. It's okay."

His heart dropped. She thought he was dismissing their kiss like it was nothing, that he intended to drop her like *she* was nothing. Like he was exactly as his reputation in town made him out to be. Irritation welled up inside him and he tried to keep his voice calm, but his reply was clipped and had her nervously glancing in his direction. "Don't do that."

"I'm sorry?" She looked confused as she diligently scrubbed an unseen spot off his counter with a washcloth.

"Don't act like you know what I was going to say."

"Oh…" He saw remorse flood her face and he regretted making her feel bad.

"I just wanted to say…" He rubbed a hand through his hair and then nibbled his bottom lip a minute as he thought before speaking again. "I've got a lot going on right now. Work, Jarin… I just…"

"And I told you I understand. We're good. Don't worry."

"No, you're not understanding because you won't let me finish." His annoyance seeped through in his tone. "Just stop thinking I'm trying to break things off with you. I'm not. I don't want to, I mean. I'm just trying to ask you for some patience with me. With all of this." He motioned towards the bathroom. "Look, I have feelings for you, okay. Like… real feelings." He tapped his heart and then watched as uncertainty flooded her blue eyes. "I'm bad at this. See, this is why I'm bad at relationships. I can't say what I mean. I stumble like a fool and then get left behind." He shook his head to clear his line of thought. "Alright, let me try this again. Erase everything I just said, okay?"

"Okay." She turned, an amused smirk on her lips as she crossed her arms and waited for him to continue. "I don't want to screw this up. You're special to me, to this town. If we try something, as in more than friends, and it doesn't work out, we run the risk of messing up some things."

"I doubt the town of Piney will suffer the consequences of a breakup, should it happen."

"If Piney lost you, Jamie, it would devastate a lot of people."

"And why would they lose me?"

"Because you'd leave. If we don't work out and you leave, everyone will be mad at me for running you out of town."

"Again, why would I leave?"

"Because you will. They all do."

"They?"

He stuttered as he realized what he'd just voiced out loud and his face blanched.

She smiled tenderly at him and walked towards him. "Okay, so you listen to me now, Jason Wright, okay?"

He nodded, words escaping him as she grabbed his hands in hers and brushed her fingertips over the calluses on his palm. She glanced up at him. "I'm not going anywhere. And if this is you saying you would like to see where things between us might head, I would like that." Her shy smile weakened his knees, and his free hand gently tucked her hair behind her ear. "You need to stop being so hard on yourself. And so do I. I know that too. Maybe we can help each other with that. And maybe we'll be just what each other needs... and wants." He cupped her face and kissed her forehead, the sounds of Jarin making racecar noises in the bath drifting through the house. "I'm a patient person. Take your time acclimating to your new role as dad. I understand if you need time and space to do that. I'll be where I always am."

"Red, you're melting me, sweetheart," he mumbled before he kissed her sweetly on the lips. It was brief, yet soft, enough of a promise to let her know he was serious but that he also didn't want to lose himself in the moment again. Yet.

"I should head home." Jamie walked to the bathroom, and her voice telling Jarin goodbye was cheerful and sweet. "I'll see you bright and early in the morning?"

"Oh, right, the food. Yes. Yes, I will be there. Billy Lou plans to get here at five, so it will be a few minutes later than our usual time." He walked her out to her car, and she opened the door, his hand resting on the top of the window.

"I look forward to it." She beamed at him, and he stepped towards her once again to brush his lips over hers. "How am I supposed to leave if you keep doing that?"

He chuckled and rubbed a nervous hand over his jaw. "You're right." He shrugged. "I just can't stop. I've wanted to for a while now."

She shook her head in disbelief at his statement. She still didn't realize how much he'd grown to care for her. "Oh, and I realize I'm now... well, I come with more than just myself now." Jason motioned over his shoulder. "So, I understand if you need some time too, to think about—" He pointed to himself and then to the house again.

She waved away his concerns with a wide smile. "I think I like the bundle deal just fine."

Relief flooded through him. "Well, I better get back to bath time. He tends to splash bubbles out of the tub if I don't pop in and supervise here and there. He has like two inches of water, and he can still manage to soak the floor with splashing. I don't get it."

"Welcome to toddlerhood," Jamie laughed. "I'll see you tomorrow, Jason."

He leaned forward and kissed her again. "Mm Mm Mmm, Red. I can't get enough. Get out of here now or I'll never let you leave." He winked as she slipped into her car. He waved as she backed out, his spirits lifted, his heart warm, and his nerves settled. He, Jason realized, had just lost his heart to Jamie Bishop.

CHAPTER TEN

Jamie had floated home on cloud nine the night before. Her lips still tingled from Jason's kiss, and she couldn't quite believe the entire evening had actually happened. But when he'd waltzed into the coffee shop this morning, he'd been his usual, charming, handsome self, and he'd planted a long, satisfying kiss on her lips before he left. It was real. Jason Wright was wooing her, and she basked in it. The bell above the door jingled and Reesa stepped through, Clare hot on her heels. Jamie's smile gave her away and Reesa began dancing the last few steps towards the counter and singing an old Marvin Gaye song that had Jamie blushing from toe to head. She swatted a hand towel towards her best friend and then giggled.

"Good morning," Reesa greeted. "Or should I say, *great* morning?"

Clare smirked as Jamie's hands flew into action to avoid Reesa's pointed stare but to also whip together their usual drinks.

"Well, how'd it go at Jason's?" Reesa asked. "Clearly there's some juicy tidbits you need to share."

Jamie turned in mock surprise. "Reesa Tate, shame on you. You know I don't kiss and tell."

Reesa and Clare both squealed as they bounced from one foot to the other in unison.

"He kissed you?!" Reesa twirled in a circle.

"Is he a good kisser?" Clare asked, and then flushed at her mother's surprised expression. "What? He's cute."

Reesa burst into laughter as Jamie did and Jamie nodded, her smile bursting forth as she held her hands to her flaming cheeks. "I still can't really believe it."

"Did you guys talk about... a relationship?" Reesa asked.

Jamie nodded. "We're taking it slow, obviously, because he has a lot on his plate, new changes, and the like. But yeah, we're going to give it a go."

"And you feel comfortable with him? With his past?"

"I do." Jamie nodded. "We all have a past, and I like that he's somewhat part of mine. And maybe now my future, too."

Clare accepted her drink and then toasted towards Jamie. "He's hot, Jamie. Good job."

Reesa swatted her daughter's arm playfully and Clare shrugged. "He's nice, too," she added for emphasis.

Jamie laughed and then her face grew serious. "Oh, speaking of cute, handsome boys, we bumped into Teddy at the grocery store last night."

Clare's eyes grew serious. "Yeah? How was he?"

"Miserable," Jamie admitted. "And the girl he was with... she was interesting."

"That's a nice way of putting it." Clare rolled her eyes.

"He told me to tell you 'nice truck.'"

Clare harrumphed then and nabbed a cookie off the tray Jamie had yet to plate and bit a mouthful before walking over to her favorite spot. Jamie looked to Reesa in concern and Reesa shrugged. "He still hasn't made any attempt of reaching out to her."
"His loss."

"Definitely," Reesa agreed.

"Oh." Jamie jumped to her feet and disappeared into her studio. She walked back out and flipped her canvas to face Clare. The teen's face split into a radiant smile as she stared at the portrait of her and her new truck.

"Jamie! This is amazing!" Clare jumped to her feet and hugged her tightly.

"I'm glad you like it. Now cheer up, sunshine, because you're awesome."

Clare laughed as she sat and admired her new painting.

"Thanks for that." Reesa hugged her.

"Well, tell me about your evening. How were things with your mom?"

"Tense," Reesa stated. "But better. She seemed attentive and eager to know Clare, which was the whole point. She even laughed a few times. I can't tell you how long it's been since I've heard my mom's laugh. So that was nice." Reesa smiled. "We are going to make an effort at meeting up every couple of weeks."

"Good." Jamie reached across the counter and squeezed her hand. "Proud of you."

"Sorry I called you in a panic."

"Don't be. That's what friends are for. I almost called you a couple of times because Jason had me so twisted up inside last night." Jamie flushed. "I wasn't sure… well, I just didn't even know what to do with myself. I felt like I was in a dream all night."

"Mr. Wright." Reesa shook her head with a sly smirk. "And people warned me about him when I first moved here. When all along they should have been warning you." She winked at Jamie and Jamie relished the joy that seeped through her.

"He thinks I'm beautiful."

"Because you are," Reesa stated as if pointing out the obvious. "And I'm glad he said so. I knew he was smart."

Jamie guffawed as Billy Lou and Charlie walked inside the shop, Jarin holding Billy Lou's hand until he saw Jamie. He sprinted towards the counter and waved up at her. "Hey there, Jarin! Good morning!"

"Daddy not here," he said by way of greeting.

Jamie smiled. "I know, but he stopped by earlier, and you know what he asked me to do?"

The boy shook his head.

"He asked me to give you this." She scooped a big cinnamon roll onto a plate and slid it across the counter to the little boy whose wide eyes soaked in the sweet deliciousness.

"What do you say?" Billy Lou asked.

"Tank you, Damie."

"You're so welcome, buddy." She beamed up at Billy Lou and Charlie.

"That's a smile of a woman in love," Billy Lou whispered to Reesa, her voice carrying enough for Charlie to excuse himself to go sit by Clare, so as not to be in the conversation. Clare excitedly showed him her new artwork.

"I'm not in love," Jamie clarified. "Yet."

"Ah, but you are well on your way. And I dare say, so is Jason. He was a jumbly fool this morning when I got to his house for Jarin. He couldn't stop jibber jabbering about y'all's supper last night and his eyes danced each time he said your name. Honey, he's half in love with you already." Billy Lou paid cash for coffee and yelled, "Charlie, your cup is ready." The older gentleman walked back over and retrieved his coffee from Billy Lou's hand, kissing her on the cheek in the process. The older woman gleamed at the attention and watched him walk back to Clare.

"And that right there is the look of a woman in love," Jamie stage-whispered to Reesa.

Reesa sighed. "We all are at some level, I think." She looked to her daughter. "Except one."

"Her time will come," Billy Lou stated. "Teddy Graham will either come to his senses, or she'll be swept off her feet by someone else. She's young. Plenty of time."

"Well, everyone is here but Theo." Reesa pouted a moment before whipping out her cell phone. "It's Saturday, he can afford to take a couple of hours off to come hang with his family."

The bell above the door jingled and Jason walked into the shop. Jamie's face lifted into a surprised smile. He noticed Jarin and the little boy ran up to him in excitement. The joy on Jason's face at his son's reaction to him had him lifting the boy up into his arms as high as he could reach before settling him on his side.

"What are you doing here?" Jamie asked. "You just left a couple of hours ago."

"And I realized that my crew is more than capable of handling a day's work without their boss hovering over their shoulder. Besides I'd much rather be here with you guys." His eyes held hers for a moment before he tickled his son's belly.

"Well now I'm definitely going to beg Theo." Reesa called instead of texted. "Hey, my dreamy grease monkey."

Jason chuckled at her sweet-talk and then stepped towards Jamie's counter, ignoring a nosy Billy Lou as she pretended to stir sugar into her coffee. "I... I already missed seeing you," he admitted quietly.

Jamie's heart squeezed at the affection in his eyes, and she relished that they were only focused upon her.

"So, let Mike fix it," Reesa complained. "Your hot, gorgeous, temperamental fiancé is begging you to come see her. I think he would understand." Reesa's voice carried to them, and Jamie giggled.

"Poor T.J. That woman has flipped his world upside down," Jamie whispered.

"I can understand that." Jason winked at her as he carried Jarin over towards Charlie and Clare. Clare animated for the young boy, and they became fast friends, his giggles flooding the room.

"My, my, my..." Billy Lou beamed. "I believe, Ms. Bishop, that we have finally completed our little family."

Jamie admired the people across the room, and grinned even bigger when she saw Theo's long legs traipsing up the sidewalk to come and enjoy time with everyone as well. When he entered, she nodded a welcome. "I think so, too, Billy Lou."

Billy Lou patted her hand. "You realize that woman is going to come back one day."

Jamie nodded. "How could she not? I'm surprised she hasn't already. That little boy is a gem. I can't imagine giving him up, and I've known him but a few days."

"She won't stand a chance in court due to her letter, but I imagine she will fight dirty one day. You prepared for that? Do you want that?"

"I want him," Jamie admitted, her eyes focusing on Billy Lou. "I think I always have, and I'll stand by him come what may."

"Atta girl." Billy Lou winked at her as she slipped away to go sit by Charlie. Jamie escaped her place behind the bar and walked towards her sign on the door and flipped it. She wanted to bask in the moment as well.

Jason glanced up at the seriousness on her face and walked her direction, his hand sliding down her arm to thread his fingers with hers. Theo's gaze followed the contact and his brows lifted, his eyes meeting Jamie's. She blushed and then turned her attention back to Jason. "Everything alright, Red?"

She forced a smile. "Yes. Just enjoying everyone here." He kissed her softly on the lips, the room quieting behind them. She ignored the stares and the sly smiles from her friends as she focused on the electric blue eyes in front of her.

"Okay you two," Reesa called. "Come enjoy some spoils." Jamie laughed at the plate of cookies Reesa had collected and brought to the table. "You can drool over one another later. Geez, these people. We can't go anywhere." Reesa looked at Theo in feigned annoyance, and he smirked before squeezing her knee and kissing her long and thoroughly.

"Well, I'm not about to be outdone." Charlie snatched Billy Lou around the shoulders and dipped her, kissing her soundly on the lips.

"Come on, Jarin." Clare stood and tugged on the little boy's hand. "Let's go. Grownups are gross."

Reesa playfully shoved her daughter's shoulder as she passed by, and Clare giggled as she took the boy to a stack of coloring books at a small table.

"Love looks good on all of us." Reesa beamed at the flush to Jason and Jamie's cheeks at her statement. "And I don't want to break up this fun, but shouldn't you boys be getting back to building my carwash?"

Laughing, Jamie sat in a free chair as the men joined in conversation and she helped herself to a cookie alongside Reesa and Billy Lou.

^

He'd spent half the morning at Java Jamie's enjoying quality time with his friends. He hadn't done that in years. Never really had the friends to do that with. Now he stood on his porch looking out over his family's land in pure contentment. Jarin napped in his guestroom, which would soon be transformed into his own bedroom, complete with a racecar bed. That was his project for next week. But for now, he'd sit on his porch and enjoy the afternoon. His cell phone buzzed, and since he did have two crews working for the day, he made sure to be on call. He glanced at the caller id and his gut dropped to his knees. Janessa. He answered with a silent plea that she hadn't changed her mind. "Hello."

"I didn't think you would answer." Her voice drifted through the line. "How is he?"

Jason rubbed a hand through his hair and sighed. "He's fine. I'm surprised you care."

"That's not fair," Janessa's voice barked. "It's because I care for him that I left him with you."

"Right. So, get to the point then, Janessa. Are you regretting it? Are you wanting him back? Because I'm here to tell you right now, you can't have him."

The line was quiet a moment and a sniffle carried through the phone. "Just love him, okay."

"I will. I do already." The depth of that love for his son after such a short time flooded through him. "I just don't want trouble for him. I don't want to be in some tug of war with you over the next sixteen years."

"You won't be. I won't... bother you again. I just wanted to make sure he was okay."

"He is."

"Good."

"Even with a thousand years, I don't know if I could ever figure out why you left him, Janessa. Are you sick? Are you dying? I mean, is it something with your health that has you wanting to see about him and secure his future? Or are you just selfish? I just can't fathom it."

"I'm fine. I told you... I'm not cut out to be a mother. I never wanted to be."

"You seem to care somewhat if you're calling me."

"I do care. I'm not a monster."

Debating that in his head, Jason exhaled. "Look, I don't know what the right move is here. I don't trust you as far as I can throw you, but I also don't want to deprive Jarin of his mother. If, and I mean *if* there's some small piece of you that wishes to stay in touch or to at least receive information about him as he grows, tell me now, and we'll make that work. But if you say no to my offer, that's it. No contact. Ever. I'm leaving the choice to you."

The quiet passed for a full minute before she said. "No. He's yours."

Jason hung up immediately, severing the tie. He had his answer. And though he did not understand it, he didn't want to prolong the conversation anymore. There was nothing she could say now. Absolutely nothing. He turned his head at the sound of a truck driving up his dirt road and stood to his feet as Charlie pulled to a stop. He rolled down his window and extended a hand containing a small white envelope. "Delivery."

Jason thumbed open the letter and read the small card, his right brow slightly tilting upward into his hairline. "What's this about?"

Charlie smirked. "Billy Lou wants everyone over at the house tomorrow. Her house. Five. Don't be late."

"Sure is a fancy supper invite. When she told me to start coming on Sundays, I didn't realize the invite came with embossed lettering."

"She wants this one to be special." Charlie smiled. "Oh, and uh... you still interested in my place?"

"I was, but Jamie said she was thinking about it, so I didn't want to interfere with whatever you two had already negotiated."

"I hear ya. Well, I'll chat with her about it again."

"Ready to say goodbye to the country?"

"Just looking for a change of scenery."

"I understand that. If she turns you down, let me know."

"Will do." Charlie tapped his temple in farewell, turning his truck back in the direction he'd come.

Jason looked at the invitation and Billy Lou's neat penmanship and the embossed lettering on the front that read "A Special Invite." He wondered what the woman had up her sleeve, but instead of wasting precious quiet time while Jarin napped on deciphering Billy Lou, Jason sent a text to Jamie about accompanying him to supper tomorrow evening at Billy Lou's. His phone dinged and she'd sent a picture of her own invitation. Curious, Jason walked inside his house to find Jarin standing in the hallway, tears falling down his face.

"Hey, buddy. What's wrong?" Jason knelt in front of the boy and Jarin dived into his embrace, his face pressed against Jason's neck.

"I scared."

Jason rubbed a hand over the boy's soft hair and nudged his face back to look at him. "Of what?"

"You left."

Jason's heart sank. "Oh, no buddy. I was just sitting on the front porch. Mr. Charlie came by and brought us this." He held the card out to his son. "We have plans with Ms. Billy Lou tomorrow for supper. Would you like to eat at her house?"

Jarin nodded, his head laying heavily against Jason's shoulder. He lifted the boy in his arms and walked over to his recliner. "Here, how about we sit here and rock for a bit." Jason eased into the chair and Jarin nestled into the crook of his arm, sighing comfortably as Jason spread a blanket over the top of them. Less than five minutes later they both snoozed.

CHAPTER ELEVEN

Jamie met him in the driveway of Billy Lou's house as he pulled in and parked next to Theo's truck. Clare's bright red pickup parked along the street in front of Jamie's car. She opened his back door and began helping Jarin from his carseat before even saying hello. "I see how it is," Jason murmured, causing her to blush. He leaned towards her and she accepted his kiss with a touch of shyness. "Good to see you, Red."

"You too. The gang's all here. Well, except Billy Lou and Charlie."

"Where are they?"

"They said they'd be back in a half hour and for us to meet them outside under the gazebo." She shrugged her shoulders. "None of us know what they're up to."

"Interesting." Jason held Jarin's hand as they walked towards the house. "Charlie talk to you about his house?"

"No. Why?"

"He mentioned he was ready to move and offered it to me, but I recalled your deal with him, and your apartment and he seemed like he would be talking to you again about it."

"Oh." She smiled in her bubbly manner. "I guess if he does, he does."

"You still want it?"

"Possibly. I'm still trying to figure out if it's the best move for me financially. Right now, my cost of living is pretty cheap. Renting a big house might be too much to take on." She paused a moment and admired Billy Lou's decorative pots and overflowing flower beds. The woman certainly had a knack for plants.

"What if you had help?" Jason asked.

She eyed him curiously. "What?"

"I mean, what if you had help with the rent? Would you want it then?"

"I wouldn't accept help with the rent, even if it is a sweet offer." She patted his arm in thanks, and he tugged her hand to stop their forward progress.

"What if it came with strings attached?"

"Those are exactly the kind of offers people stay away from most of the time." She looked confused and he brushed his thumb over her knuckles.

"What if I told you that..." He paused. "This isn't the time for this conversation," he murmured. "But... here it goes. Jamie Bishop, I want to marry you."

Her jaw dropped at his statement along with her stomach as butterflies began dancing and her knees felt weak.

"Jason, we've only really been seeing each other a few days. It's a bit quick to—"

"No. It isn't. Look, I've been down the marriage road before... twice. And I know that doesn't really make me sound appealing right now, but bear with me. I know what marriage, and the want of it, isn't. I've jumped into it before. Once I jumped quickly. The second I took my time. The difference in time meant nothing for the success of them. What wasn't there was true commitment and love. I've grown to see that over the years. What I feel for you, the promise of what we have, and what I want to give you—" He held a hand to his heart. "Jamie, I've never felt this way about anyone. I know I've got a rusty track record, and I know I don't have much to offer you, but I do have patience. So yeah, if this sounds crazy to you, then I'll wait. If you want to wait six months, a year, two years... I'll wait. I'll put in as much time as you need before you're comfortable with the idea, because I want you. I've been so blind all these years. You're my hidden ruby here in Piney. I distracted myself with diamonds, when all along the rarest, most magnificent ruby was right under my nose."

A tear slipped down her cheek, and he gently brushed it away, his thumb warm against her skin. She opened her mouth to respond as Billy Lou and Charlie pulled up to the house.

"You're supposed to be at the gazebo!" Billy Lou yelled, waving them out of sight before she and Charlie got out of the car.

"Best hurry." Jamie grabbed Jason's free hand and hurried around the side of the house to the backyard. She stopped before reaching the rest of their friends and looked up at him. "Yes, by the way." The words rushed out of her, and she beamed at the surprise that lit his face. She pushed a finger into his stomach. "Breathe," she giggled.

A breath whooshed out of him, and he nervously smiled. "You're sure?"

"Yes, but I agree with maybe taking a little more time and maybe not sharing the news as of yet."

"I don't know. I kind of want to shout it from the rooftops. Jamie Bishop wants to marry me!" He stepped closer to her, Jarin releasing his hand and hurrying towards Clare, allowing Jason to rest both hands on Jamie's hips. "I've fallen in love with you, Red. I think I forgot to mention that earlier."

"I like the sound of that." Jamie relished in his tender kiss before pulling away slightly. "But we don't want to steal their thunder." She nodded over his shoulder and Billy Lou, dressed in a cream-colored gown with a beaming Charlie, bounded down the sloped hill towards the gazebo, waving a piece of paper and dressed in their matrimonial best.

"They just got hitched." Jason's baffled words had Jamie bursting into laughter as the elderly couple hooted in enthusiasm at everyone's surprised expressions. "I'll be."

Theo stood in time to catch his grandmother as she leapt into his embrace and kissed him on the cheek, Charlie accepting an excited hug from Reesa and Clare.

"Maybe we will be talking to Charlie about his house sooner than we thought," Jamie whispered.

Jason's eyes held hers a moment and he winked. "I like the sound of that."

"Come on." Jamie tugged him towards the chatter of excitement and embraced Billy Lou in a tight hug and squeal. "Sneaky, Billy Lou, sneaky."

"It was time." Billy Lou stepped back and straightened her fitted gown and lightly touched the pearls at her ears as if her impeccable appearance might have faltered during her jaunt through the yard. "We were tired of waitin'. And people in town might talk and think we're crazy, but when you know it's the right step, you just take the jump." She winked at Charlie. "Besides, he's a hunk." Theo coughed an uncomfortable choke back and Reesa squeezed him around the waist in a hug, giggling at his embarrassment. Billy Lou turned and made an overly exaggerated gesture between Jason and Jamie and then Theo and Reesa. "Now it's your turn." Charlie swept up beside Billy Lou and dipped her in his arms, his lips pressing against hers before lifting her back to her feet as if she weighed nothing. The flush to Billy Lou's cheeks resonated in Jamie's heart. She knew that feeling. And as Jason's hand slid to hers, his strong fingers weaving amongst her own, that same feeling flooded through her once again.

"Now, welcome to our wedding reception." Charlie grinned as he clapped his hands and Billy Lou excitedly flipped a light switch on the gazebo and small fairy lights lit up the space. Music, soft and coming from a small speaker tucked in the flowerbed, began to play, and servers began exiting the house with covered dishes.

"Where on earth did they come from?" Reesa asked in wonder.

"When Billy Lou throws a party, she does it with such style." Clare grinned as Charlie extended a hand toward her for a dance, the teen gladly obliging.

"Well, do me the honor?" Reesa held out her hand to Jamie and Jamie shook her head.

"Not this time, friend. I think I want to wrap my arms around him instead." She tilted her head towards Jason, and he stepped forward with a radiant smile.

"Mr. Wright always slipping in with the steal." Reesa shook her head in mock disappointment as Theo stepped up behind her and slowly spun her into his arms. She sighed happily as he tugged her close and they danced a few steps away.

Jamie fit snugly against Jason, Jarin running up and hugging their legs as they swayed. She rested a hand on top of his hair before glancing up at Jason's proud smile. "Package deal, remember?"

She grinned. "Sounds perfect."

EPILOGUE

Stretching into the day, Jamie awakened to an arm tight around her middle and warmth behind her back. Jason. She relished the feel of his arms around her and the fact that she was now his wife. That they'd made a home together in the house Charlie had remodeled with Jason's help. They'd made it around seven months before jumping headfirst into marriage. Their ceremony was small, intimate, and perfect, just their parents and their closest friends here in Piney. Some people in town were still surprised at the pairing, but Jamie basked in the glow of being a newlywed and loved that she now sported the name Mrs. Wright. It had only been two months since they'd married, but every day with Jason had been sweet. Sure, they'd had their disagreements on where the couch should go, and which of their televisions would sit where, but other than insignificant details, life with Jason had been a sweet time thus far. Jarin, of course, was elated to have Jamie around more, and as she listened closely, she could hear his feet pattering down the hallway and towards her bedroom. She shut her eyes to see which parent he approached. Each morning he always woke Jason, but one day, she hoped he'd feel comfortable enough with her to awaken her. So, she waited patiently for that day to come.

"Daddy. Wake up." Jarin hoisted himself on the bed, ungracefully climbing from the foot of the bed and over her and Jason's tangled legs until he lay right in between them. Jason stirred and groaned at the early hour. Jamie shifted, turning so that she could see the both of them. Jason's eyes squinted open, and he smiled, his sleep-weighted hand ruffling his son's hair.

"Morning, buddy."

"I eat cereals with milk?"

Jamie smiled as Jason's eyes pleaded for her to see to Jarin. She tapped the boy's nose. "That sounds perfect. Why don't you go sit at the table and I will get you some?"

He scrambled out of the bed and padded down the hall. Jason had worked overtime for two weeks straight, and Jamie knew he was exhausted. She reached over and rubbed a hand up his arm, his eyes barely opening as he tugged her into his embrace. "I'm sorry. I just need a few more minutes."

"Rest. I've got to get going here soon anyway. I'll take him with me to the shop until Billy Lou picks him up. We'll come say bye before we leave."

He nodded, already falling back to sleep. She glanced at the clock, the time reading barely 5am. Clearly Jarin was to be an early bird like herself. She kissed Jason's cheek one more time before climbing out of bed and shuffling down the hall towards the kitchen. Jarin waited patiently, his bright blue eyes eager for food and attention. "You're going with me to the shop, so we're going to put your cereal in a bag and take it with us. Okay?"

He nodded. "Beewee."

"Yes, you will be with Billy Lou today. I think she and Mr. Charlie are going to take you to the zoo."

"Animals!"

"That's right." Jamie beamed as she reached out her hand. "Let's get you dressed." She followed him to his room, and they quietly slipped him into clothes, his soft whispers making her smile as he tiptoed down the hall to tell Jason goodbye. She heard the deep rumbles of Jason's voice and smiled, her stomach fluttering with now familiar butterflies at the sound. Jarin hurried back to her, and she handed him his bag of cereal. "When we get to the shop, you can have a muffin," she promised. "And some eggs."

"I not wike eggs," he reminded her.

"I know, but they help you grow big and strong."

"Wike Daddy."

"Yep, like Daddy." She buckled him into his car seat and kissed his cheek. His pleased giggle at tugging one of her curls melted her heart.

Life was great. *Her* life was great. She still had to pinch herself most days to even believe that so much had evolved over the last few months. Some of it was a blur, but the important moments were anchored in her soul. She lived in the town she loved, she worked a job she cherished, she had friends she adored, and she was married to the man of her dreams. Yes, life was great in Piney, and Jamie couldn't wait to see what the next chapter held.

KATHARINE E. HAMILTON

Continue the story with...

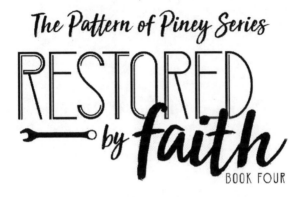

The Pattern of Piney Series

RESTORED by faith

BOOK FOUR

https://www.amazon.com/dp/B0BH4Z4D59

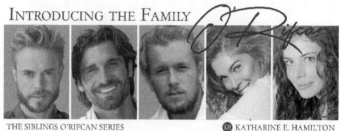

INTRODUCING THE FAMILY

THE SIBLINGS O'RIFCAN SERIES

KATHARINE E. HAMILTON

The Complete Siblings O'Rifcan Series Available in Paperback, Ebook, and Audiobook

Claron
https://www.amazon.com/dp/B07FYR44KX

Riley
https://www.amazon.com/dp/B07G2RBD8D

Layla
https://www.amazon.com/dp/B07HJRL67M

Chloe
https://www.amazon.com/dp/B07KB3HG6B

Murphy
https://www.amazon.com/dp/B07N4FCY8V

**The Brothers of Hastings Ranch Series
Available in Paperback, Ebook, and
Audiobook**

You can find the entire series here:
https://www.amazon.com/dp/B089LL1JJQ

All titles in The Lighthearted Collection Available in Paperback, Ebook, and Audiobook

Chicago's Best
https://www.amazon.com/dp/B06XH7Y3MF

Montgomery House
https://www.amazon.com/dp/B073T1SVCN

Beautiful Fury
https://www.amazon.com/dp/B07B527N57

McCarthy Road
https://www.amazon.com/dp/B08NF5HYJG

Blind Date
https://www.amazon.com/dp/B08TPRZ5ZN

**Check out the Epic Fantasy Adventure
Available in Paperback, Ebook, and
Audiobook**

U<small>THE</small>NFADING
LANDS

The Unfading Lands
https://www.amazon.com/dp/B00VKWKPES

Darkness Divided, Part Two in
The Unfading Lands Series
https://www.amazon.com/dp/B015QFTAXG

Redemption Rising, Part Three in
The Unfading Lands Series
https://www.amazon.com/dp/B01G5NYSEO

AND DIAMONDY THE BAD GUY

Katharine and her five-year-old son released Captain Cornfield and Diamondy the Bad Guy in November 2021. This new books series launched with great success and has brought Katharine's career full circle and back to children's literature for a co-author partnership with her son. She loves working on Captain Cornfield adventures and looks forward to book two releasing in 2022.

Captain Cornfield and Diamondy the Bad Guy: The Great Diamond Heist, Book One
https://www.amazon.com/dp/1735812579

Captain Cornfield and Diamondy the Bad Guy: The Dino Egg Disaster, Book Two
https://www.amazon.com/dp/B0B7QGTSFV

Captain Cornfield and Diamondy the Bad Guy: The Deep Dive, Book Three
https://www.amazon.com/dp/B0CHDDMT8M

Subscribe to Katharine's Newsletter for news on upcoming releases and events!
https://www.katharinehamilton.com/subscribe.html

Find out more about Katharine and her works at:
www.katharinehamilton.com

Social Media is a great way to connect with Katharine. Check her out on the following:

Facebook: Katharine E. Hamilton
https://www.facebook.com/Katharine-E-Hamilton-282475125097433/

Twitter: @AuthorKatharine
Instagram: @AuthorKatharine

Contact Katharine:
khamiltonauthor@gmail.com

ABOUT THE AUTHOR

Katharine started to read through her former paragraph she had written for this section and almost fell asleep. She also, upon reading about each of her book releases and their stats, had completely forgotten about two books in her repertoire. So, she put a handy list of all her titles at the beginning of this book, for the reader, but mostly for her own sake. Katharine is also writing this paragraph in the third person... which is weird, so I'll stop.

I love writing. I've been writing since 2008. I've fallen in love with my characters and absolutely adore talking about them as if they're real people. They are in some ways, and they've connected with people all over the world. I'm so grateful for that. And I appreciate everyone who takes the time to read about them.

I could write my credentials, my stats, and all that jazz again, but quite frankly, I don't want to bore you. So, I'll just say that I'm happy. I live on the Texas Coast, (no ranch living for now), and I have two awesome little fellas (ages six and two) who keep me running... literally. Though I also say a lot of, "Don't touch that." "Put that back." "Stop pretending to bite your brother." "Did you just lick that?"

Thankfully, I have a dreamboat cowboy of a husband who helps wrangle them with me. I still have my sassy, geriatric chihuahua, Tulip. She may be slowing down a bit, but she will still bite your finger off if you dare try to touch her... the sweetheart. And then Paws... our loveable, snuggle bug, who thinks she is the size of a chihuahua, but is definitely not.

That's me in a nutshell.

Thank you for reading my work.

I appreciate each and every one of you.

Oh, and Claron has now sold over 100,000 copies. Booyah!

And Graham is not far behind him.... Woooooooo!

Made in the USA
Columbia, SC
03 December 2024